"May I come in?" he asked

They had walked side by side up the narrow steps to the door of her apartment. "It isn't too late for you, is it, April?"

April shook her head and at the sound of her name she lifted her face to his. To keep her balance, she put her hands on his chest, and as she stared up into his face, her fingers curled, gathering the material of his shirt.

Russ's lips parted as though to say something else, but instead he lifted her up on tiptoes, his mouth poised just above hers. He kept her there for a second that seemed to last forever, his breath warm on her face.

"I want you to be sure, April."

"Oh, Russ," she said, "it's all right. Even if it has only been a week. I don't want to wait. Hold me."

ABOUT THE AUTHOR

Zelma Orr had a most interesting career before
turning to writing full-time: she was a U.S.
customs officer for the Treasury Department in
her home state of Texas. Zelma loves to travel
and keeps a diary of the places she has visited
to use for backgrounds in future books.

Books by Zelma Orr

HARLEQUIN AMERICAN ROMANCE

HARLEQUIN INTRIGUE

These books may be available at your local bookstore.

Don't miss any of our special offers. Write to us at the
following address for information on our newest releases.

Harlequin Reader Service
P.O. Box 52040, Phoenix, AZ 85072-2040
Canadian address: P.O. Box 2800, Postal Station A,
5170 Yonge St., Willowdale, Ont. M2N 6J3

Where Fires Once Burned

ZELMA ORR

Harlequin Books

TORONTO • NEW YORK • LONDON
AMSTERDAM • PARIS • SYDNEY • HAMBURG
STOCKHOLM • ATHENS • TOKYO • MILAN

Published October 1985

First printing August 1985

ISBN 0-373-16124-7

Chapter One

It was only a small item in the morning paper she picked up as she stopped for breakfast somewhere in northern California. It had probably been a big news story somewhere, but April didn't always see a big-city newspaper. A small-town gazette in an out-of-the-way place seldom carried a high-powered headliner.

"Hostages Held by Terrorists" was the heading midway down the front page. She shuddered. Being held anywhere against one's will was unthinkable to her. But stories such as these made the papers frequently, and it seemed to be getting worse and closer to home.

April put the paper on the table by her plate and stared out the window. It was snowing. She would avoid the twisting mountain road today and return by the route closer to the ocean highway where there was no snow accumulation.

Glancing at the truck, she smiled to see Brush curled against the window behind the driver's seat. He was a patient dog; he knew she would come back to him.

Picking up the paper again, she read the paragraph beneath the heading about the hostages. "The Allied

Region of Cyanamid Overseas Terminals, International, a U.S. firm based in Egypt, reported two engineers employed by their company had disappeared on a flight two days ago. A note delivered by mail asked for two million dollars ransom for return of the men.''

Shaking her head, April put the paper on the table and paid for her breakfast before walking out into the swirling snow. A few hours later she pulled into the parking lot of the wholesale grocery warehouse to deliver her load.

She filled out her manifests and turned them over to the consignee of the load on her truck and went to the small café she frequented when she came into the area. Someone had left a paper in the booth where she sat, and she glanced idly at the darker headings over the columns on the front page.

"ARCOT, International, Fears for Lives of Hostages." She winced. It was a San Francisco paper, and the article on the kidnapping was more detailed.

She read on. "Names of the men listed in the ransom note were disclosed this morning after next of kin had been notified. Russell Calloway..."

Her heart stopped, then raced as she read the item. "Mr. and Mrs. Thurston Calloway of Brookeville, north of Sacramento, were notified that their son was one of the men missing on the flight from..."

April put the paper down and got up from the booth, leaving without touching her breakfast. Outside, the choking in her chest eased a little as she drew in the thin cold air.

Poor Mrs. Calloway, she thought. Russ was her pride and joy. The item didn't mention a wife. After six years was Russ still searching for someone who wouldn't smother him with love? Or did his freedom mean so much to him that he wasn't interested in tying himself to one woman again?

But Russ wasn't free. He was being held hostage in a foreign country by terrorists who were not known for their love and affection.

Her return trip took all her attention as the snowstorm backtracked and covered even the southern area of her route. It was late when she left her truck in the trailer space she rented, cuddled Brush under her coat and drove her old car the few blocks to the apartment.

Her mind was on Russ, held somewhere in a foreign land against his will. Once she had held him against his will without even knowing it. She had freed him, but not willingly; nevertheless, she had finally let him go. The terrorists would not free him, not without millions of dollars paid to them by his company.

Inside the one-room efficiency apartment she called home, April looked around at the neat, uncluttered area. It would never be considered luxury, far from it, but the door locked and unlocked at her bidding. She wasn't a prisoner; she was free to come and go when she wished. Russ Calloway was not.

She eased her body onto the couch as though she might break. As a shudder passed through her, she leaned her head back to stare at the off-white ceiling, remembering the Russ Calloway she'd known years ago.

HE STOOD THERE, long arms hanging at an odd angle to his thin body. The anguish in his face was real, but

April didn't see it. She was busy denying what he was telling her.

"No, Russ, you don't know what you're saying. You—"

He turned away from her, then whirled back. "I do know what I'm saying, April. I tell you, you've smothered me. You're the only girl I've ever known. I feel like I've raised you since you were a baby."

She nodded, not understanding, refusing to understand. "Yes, I know, Russ. You're the only sweetheart I've ever had, too, but what's wrong with that?"

"Don't you see? Look at it from my point of view, April. I'm twenty-four years old, and I've never had any girl but you. There's bound to be something I'm missing by—"

Curious now, she watched him. "What do you think you're missing, Russ? I've loved you since I was twelve, and I've never thought I missed anything."

"Women are different," he told her. "They don't need the variety that men need. I want to know what it's like to associate with different types of women. I want to know how it feels not to be mothered, babied or—or handled just by you. I need to branch out and try something else."

"But—" She stopped. Something had been bothering Russ for several weeks, but she understood that going to school and working was hard on anyone. She was doing the same thing. But not this.

The full extent of what he was saying didn't filter through her consciousness, and she sat there, smiling at him, waiting for him to turn his big grin back to her. Instead, he turned away from her.

"I'm leaving, April. I'm moving out tonight." He walked out of the room and left her there. She followed him to their bedroom, watching with disbelief as he piled things into an old suitcase.

"You can't leave me, Russ. You love me, don't you?"

"I don't know anymore, April. Don't you see? I want something you can't give me. I want—"

"I don't understand. Why didn't you tell me you felt this way? We could go to a counselor. We can—"

He shook his head as he finished packing the bag with an odd assortment of his clothing he barely looked at. "I've made up my mind, April. I have to get away from you. You smother me with all your kisses, your touches all the time. I can't—I can't breathe."

April had intended the caresses as signs of affection, not bondage. She never realized Russ resented them, and she thought she knew him well.

They'd married as soon as she graduated from high school. They couldn't wait. Since her parents moved into the house next door to the Calloways when she was twelve, April had loved the handsome Russ, a very grown-up sixteen at the time. For a few years he ignored her, but one day she turned sixteen, and Russ took a good look at her. They had had eyes for no one else since that time.

Russ was right. Neither of them had dated anyone else seriously; it had always been April and Russ, Russ and April, and she'd never wanted it any other way. She thought he felt the same. Until today.

They had finished the dinner she fixed as soon as she came in from class. Noticing that he ate very little, she asked, "Don't you feel well, Russ?"

And he'd told her. Told her he was leaving. He was going to move back with his parents while he was still going for his master's degree in chemical engineering. Oh, the big dreams they'd dreamed when he got his degree and accepted a great job with one of the companies already seeking his signature on a contract for an overseas job. Big pay—after all the years of struggling, after all the hard work and no play.

Russ wanted it all alone. He didn't want her to go any further with him.

April followed him to his parents' home, hoping they could persuade him to stay with her. To her surprise they already knew Russ was planning to leave her; she was the only one who was ignorant of his feelings.

His parents, whom she'd always considered her dearest friends, were no help. They had been her parents, too, since she married Russ three years ago and her own parents had died.

"Perhaps Russ is right, April," Mrs. Calloway said. "We tried to tell you that you should wait to marry, and now you see we were right."

She stared at the handsome woman she admired more than every other woman she knew, including some of her instructors she thought were special.

"You can't mean that, Mom. You can't. I love Russ so much. How can I give him up? We've been married for three years; how can he just leave me like this?"

"I'm afraid he's made his choice, April," she said, shaking her head sadly.

She cried; she walked the floor; she swore at everyone and everything. But none of it helped, and Russ left her alone in the small apartment they'd shared for three years. Where he had carried her across the threshold after they married and made love to her for the first time—the first time for both. Where she had loved him from the depths of her being and beyond. She would have laid down her life gladly for the handsome man the young gangly teenager had become.

But she wasn't enough for Russ. She had loved him too much, held him back, kept him from lusty, growing-up experiences. He needed someone besides her.

Because she had no choice, April stayed in the small apartment with all her memories, with everything that reminded her of Russ. The smell from his shaving cream lingered days after he moved. She found odd socks that had been missing for weeks behind the cushions on the couch when she cleaned one day and sat down and cried until she couldn't breathe.

For weeks she faced each day without seeing the sunshine. She caught the same bus to class and work that she'd caught for three years, speaking to people who spoke to her, but she didn't see them. She waited for Russ to call her. He didn't call; no one called.

It was a Saturday morning two months after Russ left the apartment when April quietly went to pieces. Up until then she supposed that he'd eventually come back to her. After he had a fling with an older woman, someone more experienced, he'd come back to her. He'd realize that he could no more live without her than she could live without him. He couldn't leave her alone; she needed him.

After two months she gave up thinking he'd come back. She got up one morning and made coffee and took out the books she needed to study for her upcoming exams. But she didn't drink the coffee; the books remained closed on the table in front of her. It was the following Tuesday before one of her professors became worried about her missing classes and came by to check on her. She was lying on the couch only half-conscious and terribly dehydrated.

The psychiatrist at the hospital was sympathetic and knew the emotional vacuum that she was experiencing. But she wouldn't talk to him.

She listened. She nodded. Occasionally, she whispered, "Yes, I understand." After ten days she was released and went back to the apartment.

It smelled musty, but it still held the scent of Russ and their life together. April sat at the table with her hands folded in front of her, looking around at her three years of memories. It wasn't much, not much for having been the basis for what she thought would be a lifetime of happiness with the only man she'd ever loved or needed.

Russ needed more than her and had set out to find it. He wasn't coming back; her love was no longer the anchor that held him back. He was free to search for the experiences he wanted and had missed all those years she'd been his only love.

She got up from the table and started moving around the apartment. She changed everything.

The first thing to go was the king-sized water bed that had been their pride and joy, the only extravagant purchase they'd made since their marriage. Everything else in the apartment was from second-hand stores or Mrs. Calloway's. But the bed, where they'd shared the love April thought would last forever, was theirs.

The bed sold immediately, followed by the old overstuffed chair that Russ fitted his long body in as he studied, where he held her when he reached out to pull her onto his lap for kisses that turned into heated desire for each other. They had satisfied each other's bodies, hungry for each other, always loving. Until Russ wanted more.

The small dinette set went last. She scrubbed and cleaned out the cabinets in the tiny kitchenette, putting their mismatched plates and cups into a bag for Goodwill Industries.

She painted everything white and added pink-checked gingham curtains in her bedroom with a matching spread for the single bed she bought at the Bargain Room. Her living room/dining room/kitchen had only one window, a small one over the sink. She hung curtains with yellow tulips appliquéd along the bottom.

Eventually, the apartment looked like an entirely different place, but she could still smell Russ.

She went on to make up her exams, but once she looked at her grades, April put her books and papers aside and didn't bother to register for the fall semester.

Her part-time cashier's job was enough to support her, but without classes to keep her busy she began to look around for something else. Without a degree she couldn't apply for the job she'd wanted as consultant for an insurance firm. Somehow that didn't matter as much as she'd once thought it would; nothing mattered a whole lot.

Each day she studied the want ads. She walked miles with her mind a perfect blank. Since her stay in the hospital, she refused to dwell on the fact that Russ walked out on her. She justified his leaving with his own words: *I smothered him; now I have to let him go. He needs someone more mature than I am; he needs more experience.* Now twenty-one years old, with three years of marriage behind her, she had no experience except what Russ had given her. And that wasn't enough.

Standing in front of a torn-up portion of a building, April studied the posters showing what construction was being done. One of the posters advertised for truck drivers with their own trucks to do intrastate hauling for the company.

I think I'd like to be a truck driver, she thought, smiling to herself. *I have the education for it.* She laughed softly and turned away.

It was too early to go to bed, so she stopped at the small café where she often ate a sandwich, sitting at the counter with a cup of coffee. Not many people were in the room, and she didn't hurry.

"Well, April," Corinne said. "What are you doing out all alone tonight? Russ know you're not at home?"

She stiffened, waiting for the crushing pain to squeeze her breath from her body. Nothing happened. All she felt was emptiness, a rough emptiness as though her breath pushed around huge rocks to go from her chest to her nostrils. Corinne didn't know that Russ had left her. She hadn't told anyone.

Her voice perfectly natural, she said, "He knows he brought me up right, Corinne, so he doesn't have to worry."

The girl laughed and went on to her other customers while April stared into her coffee cup. She had survived. There was no more pain. Where the fires of her love for Russ once burned and smoldered, where red-hot coals were ignited by their love, where once the magic of her response brought him the greatest of pleasures, nothing was left. Nothing. Where fires of love once burned brightly, only black ashes remained.

April walked home slowly, hands in her jacket pockets, looking up at the cold stars of late fall. Soon the snows would come. Soon it would be Christmas. Last Christmas... Even as she thought of last Christmas with Russ, there was no pain. There was no feeling at all.

THE NUMBNESS STAYED WITH APRIL through the lonely months. Even when the telephone that hadn't rung over half a dozen times since Russ left was ringing as she unlocked the door to the small apartment.

It was Mrs. Calloway. "April?"

"Yes, Mrs. Calloway."

There was a long hesitation. "How are you, dear?"

For three months no one had wondered about her. For three months no one had called to check on her. She pressed the receiver to her ear.

"I'm fine."

Mrs. Calloway's words came out in a rush. "I wanted—that is, Russ asked me to call to tell you he's filing for divorce." She stopped. April waited.

"Russ has accepted a job overseas and will be leaving in thirty days." She waited, but April sat quietly without speaking. "April?"

"Yes."

"He's planning to send you some money because he wants you to finish your schooling. He wanted to let you know."

"Thank you, Mrs. Calloway."

Russ was doing his duty by providing money for the completion of her education. He could no longer give her love, but he'd have a job that paid enough for him to help her continue her schooling.

She hung up the phone and sat there. Even as she recognized complete abandonment by Russ and his parents, she felt only bewilderment. The woman she'd loved as a mother was as much a stranger as the husband she'd loved to the exclusion of all others for nine years, since she was twelve years old.

It was somehow frightening to realize that she could no longer feel any emotion. But it was better that way. No more hurting, no more emptiness, just nothing.

She had beaten her own defeat; she'd won. Russ was free, or he would be once the divorce was final. He had a grand job with a big company overseas as a chemical engineer. He had his freedom to love all the women he needed; to get all the experience she'd kept him from having; to have it all, now that April was no longer a deterrent.

During the weeks she read the want ads, she'd filled out an application for a job with the United Parcel Service, delivering merchandise part-time in the evenings. When they called her in for an interview, she was surprised that they hired her, because she was a female and not a very big one at that. But the job helped. It helped to keep her occupied so she didn't sit and stare into space. It got her out of the apartment and took her to parts of town where she'd never been. She met strangers and talked to them without hearing much of what was said.

It was the week of Thanksgiving that the first check arrived from Russ. It had been mailed to the Calloways, and they, in turn, mailed it to April so she wouldn't know where he was, she supposed. It didn't matter to her; she deposited the check to her account and forgot about it until the next one came just before Christmas.

In that envelope with the check a note was enclosed from Russ. She stared at the familiar handwriting, thinking, *How nice of him*.

He'd written: "April—"not even "dear" in front of it.

I was lucky and landed a good job. Please use the money any way you want to, but I'd like to see you finish your education. I know how hard you've worked toward your degree, and you deserve it.

Russ.

But that was all she deserved, according to Russ. What about his love?

Wadding the note into a tight ball, April pitched it into the wastebasket. The check went into her growing bank account.

Papers showing she was divorced arrived from a lawyer a year after Russ moved out of her life. She read them through without understanding any of the legal terms except that she no longer had any claim on Russ; he was free to spread his wings and fly; fly away from her to a wider experience than she could give him.

She, too, was free, a single woman no longer bound to the man who didn't need her. A judge in municipal court reinstated her maiden name for the small fee of fifty dollars. She was now April Hayden, no longer April Calloway. She wrapped her wedding rings in tissue paper, packed them in a box and mailed them to Russ in care of the Calloways.

Checks from Russ continued to come addressed to April Calloway, and she deposited them to her account. For two years they arrived, until he assumed she'd finished her schooling; then they stopped coming.

When the checks stopped, she moved from the small apartment where she had remained since he left her. She not only moved from the apartment, but left the small town thirty miles north of Sacramento to move into the southern edge of the larger city, fifty miles from the Calloways.

Not that it mattered. She didn't see or hear from any of them.

Her new apartment was a furnished efficiency contained in one room. It had a couch that made into a bed, a small refrigerator and an even smaller gas range that she never used except to make coffee. She didn't need room in a place she used only as a turnaround, a place where she did her laundry, inventoried her clothing and paid rent once a month.

Her experience with United Parcel Service was enough to convince her she loved driving a truck, and instead of going back to get her college degree, she took the money Russ sent and invested it in a van. Her advertisement that she'd do intrastate hauling netted her plenty of business to keep her on the move. After a year she bought a truck rig and expanded her territory to include the entire state of California.

Being on her own had taught her how to manage, had given her a little insight into what it took to operate in the black when it came to dealing with money. Nothing had prepared her for the mumbo jumbo she faced when she applied for licensing of a vehicle for private enterprise.

Special titles for taxes, special insurance rates, special license tags all took time and a lot of running from place to place.

And, of course, the questions when a *female* applied for a commercial trucking permit.

"You gonna drive a sixteen wheeler?" the burly sergeant at the license bureau asked.

"Yes." April's eyes glinted with amusement as he stared at her, shaking his head as he bent to fill out the long forms with several sets of numbers. He muttered something about women in men's jobs and went off to get the application certified.

Necessary papers were finally filed and copies distributed where needed. Freedom to move was hers as she found that shipping by truck, when dependable, was a commodity cherished by small businesses.

She was a legitimate truck driver, and she became known to others as she made her deliveries and frequented the truck stops for coffee and meals. Eventually, even with all the teasing about a female trucker, she was accepted. She was a hard worker, offered no real competition for their cross-country lines and stayed in her territory; she was dependable.

The men liked that. She didn't ask for favors. If her rig needed looking after, she took care of it herself. A flat tire offered no more of a challenge for her than it did for a two-hundred-pound man once she learned the right way to do it.

After weeks on the road with no one to talk to except herself, April stopped one day at a home for stray animals and walked through the pens. At the last pen lay a small terrier type, his sad brown eyes watching her disinterestedly.

"What's wrong with him?" she asked the caretaker.

The man looked at the dog where she pointed and shook his head. "Guess someone lost him or else dropped him off around here. He came in without a collar or tags. Have to get rid of him soon."

"Get rid of him?"

"We only keep them five days if no one claims them."

She turned back to look at the dog. "How old would you say he is?"

"Couple of years. Well trained. It's a shame." He walked away from her to take care of his other duties.

"Don't just lie there; get up and come over here where I can pet you," she told the sad-eyed dog.

He didn't move for a moment, then, slowly, his stubby tail began to wag. April moved closer.

"Come on," she entreated, sticking her fingers through the wire. After a bit, he dragged himself forward enough to lick her fingers, and when she scratched behind the pointed ears, he put his nose to the wire.

I'm probably asking for trouble, she thought, *but we need each other. He has a good many years left, and I need someone besides me to talk to on the road.*

So Brush became a part of her life. The name came from the short coat, almost like wire, that had to be brushed to within an inch of his life after she took him home and bathed him. He was some kind of fox terrier with a thin, tight body that he carried proudly.

The sad brown eyes became bright, mischievous signals of when he was about to tease her into playing with him. His long squared-off nose was black, and part of that black encircled half of one eye, giving him a cockeyed look. The other eye was circled in brown, and the rest of his body was mixed brown, black and white. He was adorable, and he grew to love the truck just as she did, knowing when he climbed into the seat beside her that it meant a long ride. He slept by the window behind her or on the seat beside her, but he went everywhere she went.

And no matter how much she loved and petted him, Brush did not complain; the more she loved him, the more he adored her.

The love she had for Russ was tucked into a corner of her heart, out of the way, where she wouldn't stumble over it, where it no longer suffocated her to think about it, where it no longer stifled Russ. The ashes left over from where fires once burned stayed cool, with no heat to remind her of what had been.

Russ seldom surfaced in her thoughts after all the years of running from him over the highways of California. He was somewhere in the distant past, and she was way ahead of him, traveling her own road.

Occasionally, at one of the truck stops where she was a familiar figure, she shared a beer with other drivers. And as it sometimes happened, someone made a pass at her. She laughed it off, and that was as far as she allowed it to go. She slept alone, as she had since Russ left her. She didn't think about it; she just didn't want attachments of any kind.

She shared her love with Brush, not caring what anyone else thought about her standoffishness where men were concerned. Russ was right: it was nice not to have to answer to anyone but herself—and Brush.

APRIL CAME BACK to the present with a start as the music on her radio was interrupted for a newsbreak. The story of the kidnappings from the American company overseas was at the top of the newscast and included speculation as to whether ARCOT would give in to the demands for millions of dollars for the safe return of its employees and educated guesses trying to evaluate the chances of returning the men alive. Everyone had an opinion, but no one knew what would happen.

Did the company he worked for think Russ was worth a million dollars? Were two men worth two million dollars? How was life valued by a big company? By the families of the men?

Once Russ had meant all the world to April. She'd have given her life plus the few dollars they were able to save as they juggled college and jobs. Her heart had been his for so many years, she couldn't remember being without him. She gave him everything, including all the love that filled her mind, heart and soul. A human life is invaluable, and to April, Russ ranked highest in importance, monetary value notwithstanding.

His parents would be frantic. The Calloways didn't have millions of dollars to pay for Russ's life, but if they had it, they'd gladly give it all for him.

So would she. Even knowing he no longer loved her, even knowing she'd never again be able to acknowledge her love for him, if she had a million dollars, she'd give it to free Russ.

Chapter Two

Tucking Brush into the front seat of her car beside her, April left early, skirting Sacramento morning traffic on her way north to Brookeville. The streets of the small town where she'd lived most of her life hadn't changed all that much. As she turned the corner of the street where she'd lived, next door to the Calloways, she was trembling.

The Calloway house looked the same as it did ten years ago when the Haydens lived next door and the gangly April loved the handsome boy who lived there. The paint looked fresh; the lawn was pale green with the year-round grass Mr. Calloway enjoyed.

Leaving Brush in the car, she walked over the familiar sidewalk, the piece still broken from the block near the steps, up onto the small porch. She knocked and heard footsteps coming down the hall they had never carpeted.

The door opened, and Mr. Calloway looked out at her from brown eyes with dark circles underneath. His thinning hair was white instead of the black she remembered.

He stared at her, not recognizing his former daughter-in-law. "Yes?"

His voice was the same. A voice that had teased her for years as the pesty little teenager next door who became his daughter-in-law and, finally, his ex-daughter-in-law.

"Hello, Mr. Calloway," she said, refraining from using the term 'Dad' after all these years.

He didn't recognize her, but that didn't surprise April. He remembered her as a laughing, friendly, happy-go-lucky girl who loved his son beyond thought. A girl whose dark brown eyes laughed, whose nut-brown hair swung freely over straight shoulders, whose maturing body had a tendency to nurture baby fat into rounded curves that fit Russ's hand so well, a girl who loved the Calloways as her own family.

"I'm April," she said as he continued to gaze at her without any sign of recognition.

No wonder he didn't know her. Where once her body had been rounded, she was slender. The fullness of glowing young cheeks had given way to a thin face, lightly tanned from her hours on the road and out-of-doors. There was little left of the April Calloway or the April Hayden of yesterday. Six years later, she was no longer the woman they had known.

His mouth worked, and tears came into his eyes. Silently, he opened the door and motioned her inside. They looked at each other, but he made no move to touch her, and she waited.

The bare hallway was the same. To her left was the living-room door, and she could see Mrs. Calloway seated in the same rocking chair she always sat in, rocking as she sewed something in her lap.

"Mom, it's April," Mr. Calloway said.

The woman looked up at the tall, thin girl standing beside her husband, and suddenly she screamed. The material in her hands fell to the floor as she stood up and took a step toward April.

"It's your fault," she said, her words unclear as she began to cry with great heaving sobs. "You did it. You never wrote him. You moved away without an address. You left him." She wiped at her eyes and went on accusing April. "It's all your fault. You let him go."

She went on and on as April stood before her, wondering how she had ended up being the cause of Russ's trouble.

You never wanted me around, she wanted to tell Mrs. Calloway. *You said he was right and should be free to do as he wanted. Russ left me; I didn't leave him. I would never, never have left him, and you know that.*

But no words left her lips as she took in the miserable couple in front of her. They had to accuse someone; there had to be someone to bear the brunt of their inconsolable grief. They couldn't accuse the terrorists, but April was there in front of them, and she could be blamed for everything.

There was no chance to defend herself as the woman cried and shouted at her. Mr. Calloway moved to stand close, holding his wife.

"I'm sorry; really sorry," April said. "If there's anything at all that I can do..."

Blank eyes didn't acknowledge that she had spoken, that she was even there. She turned and left.

Brush wagged a greeting as she slid into the car seat and sat looking back at the house she had just left. Her glance went to the building next door where she had lived with her parents until her marriage, where they remained until their deaths two years after she married Russ.

The neighborhood was composed of old houses, old families that took care of the property, planted flowers, kept the yards clean, painted the outsides as well as the insides of their homes to keep them in good repair.

It didn't seem like home anymore. She had been gone nine years, and she was a stranger in a strange suburban area. Looking back at the house occupied by the Calloways, she frowned. The last time she had been there, the mantel held pictures of a laughing young couple, her and Russ—the senior prom, graduation day, their wedding day. All the pictures had been removed. Only one picture of Russ had been on the mantel. Russ in a business suit, standing by a plane, carrying a briefcase.

He was older than when last she saw him, so it must have been on one of his trips home from the great job he had with ARCOT, International. His features were no longer boyish; he wore his hair shorter than she remembered. Only his eyes seemed the same—bright blue beneath bushy light brown brows and darker brown lashes. He was handsome, but no longer the handsome boy she remembered. He had grown into a distinguished-looking chemical engineer for ARCOT, with no one to answer to except himself and perhaps his employer.

Were there a lot of other women for him? Had he found the variety and experience she couldn't give him? She guessed that he must have in six years. If there was no wife—

When April finally pulled out of the driveway, Brush settled once more contentedly beside her. Her thoughts went back to the Calloways. They seemed so much older than when she last saw them, but then, so did she. Six years older. Six years of experience all alone, without Russ, with whom she started out. Would he be interested in her with age and experience behind her?

Now there were lines near her eyes, dark brown eyes that seldom laughed anymore. Shoulder-length nut-brown hair was bell shaped, blunt cut, without the full bangs she once sported, brushed away from her face. There were strands of gray mixed in the thickness she hid with the cap she wore. It didn't bother her.

"What experience?" she asked herself aloud, and laughed softly. "Truck driving, Brush. That's where my experience has been. I really don't think that would count for the type any man might be looking for."

Her next schedule was for early tomorrow morning—a trip up north hauling cattle feed to a ranch just beyond Susanville, across the Stover Mountain Range. She liked that drive. North on Interstate 5 to U.S. Route 36, where she would head east; it was beautiful. The snow had diminished a lot in the past few weeks, so the roads were clear. Hopefully, they'd stay that way until after the weekend, when she'd be back home.

It was late enough to eat her evening meal, and if she went by the truck stop, she could catch the news while she ate. Not owning a TV set didn't bother her at all, but she did like the news program Elsa usually turned on at about dinnertime.

"Come on, Brush," she said. "You need to stretch your legs a bit before I go inside. I promise to bring you some bones Elsa's been saving for me." They walked across the parking lot to a grassy-stripped median, and she waited as the little dog sniffed around.

A diesel horn blasted, and she turned to wave at Wade Outen as he pulled out of the parking area behind the truck stop on his way to Salt Lake City, his normal route. He was one who made it a habit to ask her out at least once a month, undaunted by the fact that she turned him down just as regularly.

"One of these days, April," he told her, grinning, showing straight white teeth, "you're gonna forget your habit of automatically shaking your head when I get close to you and you'll say yes."

"You could be right, Wade," she said, and let it go at that. She didn't make excuses for not going out with anyone; she just said no. She didn't really know why herself; she didn't even try to figure it out. It wasn't loyalty to Russ, to a marriage long since dissolved, to a man who didn't care. It was disinterest.

With Brush safely back in the car, April went inside and found a booth not too far from the TV set sitting above the counter. The news was just coming on as she ordered and sat back in the booth to watch.

Weather was tops in the news in much of the Northeast and Southeast. Late-season snowstorms in the Midwest turned into rampaging flash floods through Pennsylvania and parts of New York, through Louisiana and northern Florida.

Her meal was served, and she smiled at the young girl working as waitress—Katie, one of Elsa's daughters, working after school.

"ARCOT, International today informed the news agency that demands for ransom had been met for the two engineers held hostage for twelve days."

Her fork clattered to the plate as she looked up at the TV screen. An inset picture of Russ and an older man flashed for a brief moment on the set, then another man, evidently a spokesman for ARCOT.

"They have been released and are expected to arrive in neutral territory at any time; possibly Cairo, but we aren't positive of that location."

The newscaster asked another question she didn't hear, and the ARCOT man took a moment before he answered.

"Our contact said only that they would be returned to neutral territory immediately. Both men are said to be in good physical condition."

The rest of the newscast passed unnoticed as April finished her meal, absorbing only the fact that Russ was reportedly safe. The news media were very careful to use words like "reportedly" and "anticipated" instead of saying it's a true fact or that it would definitely happen.

No matter. They *said* he was all right. It was enough for the moment. Perhaps Mr. and Mrs. Calloway had already been notified that they believed Russ would be returned to his company unharmed.

As she paid her check, she asked Elsa behind the cash register, "Got any goodies for Brush? I sort of promised him some."

Elsa, looking as if she ate her share of profits from the menu of the truck stop, laughed. "Sure. Just waiting for you to come by." She disappeared through the swinging doors, only to reappear almost immediately with a big package wrapped in brown paper.

"Here you are. Enough to last him a day or two."

"Good. That's how long I'll be gone," April told her.

"Where to this time?"

"Susanville. Be back Saturday late."

"Be careful," Elsa warned her, just as she always did, waving as she left.

Brush was waiting for her, too. "You'll just have to wait till I get home," she told the little dog. "Too messy to eat in the car."

Once Brush was fed and his wiry coat untangled a little with a stiff brush, April fixed the couch into a bed and found a book she had started. Between the pages and her eyes, Russ's face suddenly appeared. Not the way he looked now but the way he was when she loved him. For many years his face was the only one she saw. It had taken all this time to remove him from her consciousness, to push his image away each time it appeared. A long time, but she had finally rid her mind of the features seemingly engraved there.

Now in the national news headlines, Russ was back to haunt her. She closed her eyes shut, then focused on her book, but no matter how hard she concentrated, she couldn't see past the specter.

PARKING HER CAR in the back of the trailer lot, April checked around her rig she had ready to go. She cleaned the windshield and her rearview mirrors, and hung a change of clothing in back of her. It was still dark as she pulled out onto the interstate. The weather report was good; there should be no problem.

Beside her, Brush curled into a ball and continued his interrupted sleep. Through the sleeping city, she guided the big rig; it wasn't as heavy as some she pulled and was much easier to handle. A hundred miles later, she made the turn east that would take them across the mountains. The second hundred miles, which took her into Susanville after crossing the mountain range and gearing down for the descent on the opposite side, was slower.

Even though it wasn't late when she delivered the trailer at its destination, she signed for a room at the truck stop to stay until morning. Her next run wasn't until Monday, and there was no need to hurry back to Sacramento.

That night, for the first time in years, she dreamed about Russ, saw him clearly as he reached to pull her to him, saw him as he laughed at something she said or did, felt his mouth on hers the way it had always been—warm and gentle.

She awakened with a start and lay there staring into the dark. How unusual. Because of the news stories, of course, and she had been worried about him. Anyone would be. She twisted in the narrow bed, finally getting back to sleep hours later.

Tired from wrestling with thoughts and dreams, she climbed into her rig and started back across Stover Mountain. No longer pulling the heavy load behind her, she could make better time on the return trip.

She had started the descent on the western slope of the mountain when Brush suddenly sat up beside her and whined. "What's the matter? Need to stop?"

Brush had certain actions he went through when he needed to stop at a comfort station, and this was not one of them. He sat up on his hind legs and put a paw on her arm, his bright button eyes imploring as he continued to whine.

She looked ahead at the road; it was clear, no traffic. They were coming to some sharp curves, but she was driving at a good rate to take them; the weather was good. She frowned, glancing back at the small dog; Brush continued to stare into her face.

"Okay," she told him. "As soon as we get to that slope that has a turnoff, I'll stop. Just a mile or so. Can you wait?"

He whined again and gave a short "woof." She took that to mean yes and turned her attention back to the road.

She was driving on the inside of the curve, close to the mountain, with sides going straight up her right, and was unprepared to meet the speeding pickup truck as it rounded the sharp turn in her lane. It came straight at her, the driver not seeing or not caring that they were on a collision course and she had nowhere to go.

Brush had warned her, but she hadn't listened. Her hard pull to the right on the wheel made only a marginal difference as the driver of the truck, seeing her at the last minute, swerved. He couldn't avoid her altogether and scraped the cab, catching the back axle of her rig. Her hands were jolted loose from the steering wheel, and she was slung forward, her left eye connecting with the hard rim.

Pain knifed through the side of her head, and stars filled the blackness for a moment, exploded and disappeared in the darkness.

The sirens came closer and dropped to a wail, but April found she couldn't raise her head to see what was happening. It hurt too much. Flexing her right hand, she slid it along the seat, trying to find Brush. Her tongue dried against the roof of her mouth as she tried to call him.

The door at her side was wrenched open, and voices called, demanding an answer she couldn't give them.

Gentle hands extracted her, and she cried out as she was lifted, letting the dimness swim over her.

From somewhere she could make out words now. "It's a girl," a man's voice said nearby. She opened her eyes to look into the face of a policeman. Sunlight glinted off his badge, and she closed her eyes again.

"Brush?" she asked, trying to free her hand.

"It's all right, ma'am," the same voice said. "You're all right."

She tried to shake her head, but the pain lit another shower of stars inside, and she lay still. "There was a little dog with me," she whispered.

"Yes, ma'am. He's fine."

She closed her eyes and stopped fighting the waves of blackness, sinking into a painless vacuum.

Chapter Three

Restlessness had driven him from the small neat house where he'd grown up. Russ's parents were pathetically glad to see him home safe, and he understood. There had been days when he thought he'd never see them again. But on those dark days his thoughts hadn't been of his parents. April was the one who came to him in dreams, who lingered beside him after he was interrogated by the terrorists, after he was beaten and denied food. Her hands touched him as he passed in and out of consciousness, her lips soft on his cheek, calling his name, whispering, "I'm here, Russ. I'll always be here."

He remembered the hijacking of his company's plane, the disbelief to find himself the object of a kidnapping, held along with Ross Winton for two million dollars. The days that followed were days he was trying to forget. Most of the time his disciplined mind could take whatever the terrorists dished out; sometimes he almost gave up. That's when he dreamed of April.

He had depended on her to be there; hers was the presence that kept him from giving up, that encouraged him to keep his sanity when his brain begged for release, any kind of release.

Now he recognized the neighborhood he was in. Making a right turn at the stoplight past the high school where he and April used to go to Friday night football games, he guided his dad's new car down a side street and stopped.

The apartment where he and April had lived was painted beige instead of gray the way he remembered it. A sharp pain in his chest made him close his eyes a moment, and when he opened them, they rested at the foot of the outside stairs. A child's tricycle lay over on its side, the handlebars resting on the second step where April used to sit and wait for him when he worked over at his part-time job.

His eyes were still on the tricycle when a small boy ran around the corner of the house. He carried a toy plane held over his towhead, zooming it through imaginary clouds, laughing with his eyes crinkled. April used to do that. Was the child hers? Whom had she married? What was she doing? Did she ever think of him?

His throat hurt. Shaking his head, he started the car and drove away from the small boy and the apartment he'd been so intent on leaving six years ago. He hadn't been able to get away fast enough, not from the small town, the small rooms, from April, whose only fault had been in loving him.

Oh, yes, he'd left it all behind in search of the American male's dream—the security of a great job and the freedom to do what he pleased, with whom he pleased. No ties that bind.

Inside the uncarpeted hallway of his parents' house, he laid the car keys on the highboy, that piece of furniture from another way of life. April had loved that particular dark walnut monstrosity and laughingly dared his mother to will it to anyone else. Who else was there? Russ was an only son and April their only daughter-in-law, so she knew it would one day be hers.

"Lunch will be ready in about fifteen minutes, Russ," his mother said as he wandered into the kitchen.

"Want me to set the table?" he asked.

"Oh, I can do—"

He interrupted her by going to the buffet to remove plates and salad dishes. He and April always rotated their chores—she cooked and he set the table and washed dishes one day, then they reversed duties the next—with lots of hugs and kisses when they passed each other. His gut churned. How long had she been married? Was the little boy her only child?

After they finished the meal, Russ followed Mr. Calloway into the living room and sat down with him as he turned on the TV set for the midday news. He dreaded this program, but he made himself watch; he'd been a part of it so much lately that he was anxious to see what else was happening in the world.

"Police are investigating an accident on the western slopes of Stover Mountain yesterday resulting in the injury of a young female truck driver. She has been identified as April Hayden of Sacramento. Doctors at the hospital where the young woman was taken say she suffered a slight concussion, cuts and bruises when her rig was forced from the road by a vehicle fleeing police."

Russ stared at the announcer. April Hayden. Did he mean April Calloway? *His* April?

"According to Elsa Maxwell of Maxwell's Truck Stop in Sacramento, Miss Hayden is a frequent visitor there, renting space for her trucking rig from them. Miss Hayden has no immediate family, she said.

He didn't know how he got out of the house, how he explained to his parents he had to talk to someone who knew April. When he left, they hadn't kept track of April because they thought it best for all concerned not to keep in touch. They knew nothing about her. He couldn't blame them; after all, he'd abandoned her. Why should they take any responsibility?

He found Elsa Maxwell with eyes glued to the TV set while she held a telephone receiver to her ear. He waited until she hung up the phone.

"Mrs. Maxwell?"

The woman who turned had been crying, her full cheeks streaked with tears. She swiped at them and sniffed.

"I'm sorry. Can I help you?"

He nodded at the TV. "Have you any other news than what they've given? My family and April's were close when they lived next door to us in Brookeville."

"I was talking to a nurse at the hospital just now. She's—April's gonna be all right. But I was so shocked." She blinked and wiped chubby fingers across her eyes. "Do you really know April? She said she didn't have any family."

"Yes, I know her," he said.

"Well, she got a lick on her head and doesn't remember who she is, but it's not supposed to be serious." She sniffed again. "If you don't know who you are, I think it's pretty serious."

Russ sat on a stool at the counter, and Elsa poured him a cup of coffee. "I—our families sort of lost track of each other," he said. "I didn't know she was driving a truck now." So April wouldn't even remember she was once married to Russell Calloway. Perhaps she'd already forgotten over the years. The familiar emptiness was back, the emptiness that came when he realized he'd given up the only woman he'd ever really loved.

"Yeah, she does and loves it. Says she wouldn't do anything else. What was she doing last time you saw her?"

"She was still going to college." He took a sip of coffee, remembering their books stacked together on the shaky old coffee table, a refugee from the Calloway attic. In the dungeon where the kidnappers held him prisoner, he'd longed for a book to hold, to look at, anything that would prove there were still civilized people in the world. He'd thought of all those ponderous textbooks April lugged to and from classes, riding the bus that was never on time.

How odd, he was thinking, that she'd drop out of college to drive a truck. On one of his trips home he'd gone down to see one of his professors at the college; as he left, he went by the registrar's office to ask when April Calloway graduated. Perhaps they'd know where she'd gone to work and he'd just drop by to see how she was doing.

The girl checking their list of graduates for the years he said might apply looked up at him. "April Calloway didn't graduate any of those semesters. Do you think she could be earlier or later?"

He couldn't even guess. "Perhaps later," he said.

She shook her head. "Let me check this one other place," she said, getting up to open a file drawer at the back. After a moment she returned with a folder.

"According to this, she dropped out after finishing her junior year."

Outside in the bright spring sunlight, he found it hard to breathe. Of all the things April wanted, aside from his love, it was her education. She worked, she went to school, she slaved over their budget, all so that they could both have an education. His parents had helped, of course, but it was April who gave her time and energy so they would survive.

But after he left her, she quit college. She *quit*. She didn't graduate as he'd wanted her to do. The girl had nothing to indicate where April might have gone to work when she left college.

Down the street, Russ found a bar and sat in a booth at the back with one drink most of that afternoon. What he'd fought against when he was married to April, he wanted back again. He couldn't forget her and the love he'd had for the teenager, developing now into desire for the woman she became.

He blinked and came back to what Elsa said as she excused herself to go down the counter to pour coffee, then returned to stand near him. "The doctor did say April could leave the hospital Monday if she's not running a fever."

"What about her truck? Is it badly damaged?" he asked, still fuzzy from his wandering thoughts.

"No. Even Brush escaped without losing any hair."

"Brush?"

Elsa laughed, a deep friendly chuckle. "April's little dog. He's an escapee from the local Humane Society."

He pushed his cup across the counter for a refill. "How will she get home?"

"Some of the truckers here were talking about it. Whoever happens to be off when they release her will go up and drive back for her."

He stayed in the truck stop over an hour, listening to Elsa and her customers talk about April. And he was jealous of the camaraderie they felt for the one female trucker in their midst.

The ten o'clock evening news was on when he got home, and he smiled at his parents as he sat near his mother. The newscaster mentioned the accident briefly, but Russ's eyes instantly became glued to the screen when a picture flashed. It was April, holding a scruffy-looking little dog. The smile on her too-thin face crinkled her dark eyes the way he remembered, thick hair swinging against her cheek. Then the picture was gone, but he still sat there, staring at the illumined screen.

"HOW MUCH DAMAGE to my rig?" April asked.

The policemen who'd pulled her from the truck were back to complete their report and were filling her in on what happened on the downhill western slopes of Stover Mountain.

"You mean you own that thing?"

"Thing?" She squinted at him from beneath the bandage over her left eye. "That *thing* is my livelihood."

The policeman shook his head. "I couldn't believe it when we pulled you out of there." He grinned. "Just a few scratches on the paint and a bent rear wheel. You were traveling with luck, young lady."

Her sore body relaxed. Brush was being cared for; the truck wasn't in too bad a shape. "And me? What kind of shape am I in except one eye doesn't work and my head is splitting?"

"I'd rather the doctor told you, but they said a mild concussion along with the cut over your eye. I guess it doesn't feel mild right now."

"You're right," she said.

A white-coated figure came through the doorway and after a few words with the policeman stood by her bed.

"Well, April, how do you feel?"

She stared at him with an odd feeling. The name didn't sound familiar at all. He was busy checking her eyes, the funnel-shaped instrument, fitted around his head, giving him direct light to look into her pupils.

"The cut is quite deep," he said as he probed gently. "But there's no damage to the eye itself. You'll have a scar that will be hidden by the brows." He straightened. "Is there still pain in your head behind the eye?"

"Yes." She continued to stare at him, wondering about the name. She remembered Brush; she didn't remember April.

"We'll get you something a little stronger for the pain, since you're conscious. It's going to hurt for a while."

"Doctor?"

He smiled. "You'll have to stay a couple of days until you can travel. I understand you're from Sacramento."

"Yes." She bit into her lip. "You called me April, but I don't remember that being my name."

The doctor, in the midst of counting her pulse, looked up quickly. "You don't remember your name?"

"Well, I don't remember April."

"What do you remember?" he asked, his hands still on her wrist.

"Brush, the little dog that was with me."

"What do you recall about the accident?"

"Just the truck coming at me."

"What were you doing on that mountain?" he asked, once more bending to shine the light into her left eye he pried open.

"I don't know." She tried, but nothing came back after the truck hit her. It was blank—before and after. "Concussions make you forget sometimes, don't they?"

"Yes," he said quietly.

"How do I remember a dog but don't remember me? I know the truck I was driving is mine, but I don't recall my name. That doesn't make sense, does it?"

"The medical profession has never been able to determine why blank spots occur in semiamnesia."

"Amnesia?" The word penetrated, and she tried to sit up. "But I can't have amnesia if I remember some things."

"This type seldom lasts long. A good sleep and a few days' rest will usually take care of it." His hand on her shoulder kept her from sitting up. "Let's not aggravate it, April. Lie still until we take another look at those X rays."

"Don't let them lose Brush," she said drowsily, and waited until he nodded before she went to sleep.

She was wide awake, and her head had stopped hurting by the time they brought her evening meal. The young girl placing the tray where she could reach it grinned at her.

"You sure did liven things up around here," she said.

"It must really be dull, then," April responded.

The girl took a few steps and turned on the TV set that was installed at an angle to the bed, tilted down so that she could see it from the propped-up position they now allowed her to use.

"The local news will be on in a few minutes. You and Brush are celebrities."

"Who has Brush?"

"One of the policemen who brought you in took him home and said he'd keep him till you get out of here. Probably a couple of days."

"I feel fine," April told her.

"Uh-huh, but you still don't know who you are."

Left alone, she ate a few bites, then lay back to watch the news program coming on. There was a story of two men, engineers with an American firm, who'd come home after being released by kidnappers in some foreign country. An unnamed amount of ransom had been paid for their release. The men, already back in the United States, were apparently unharmed.

She yawned during the commercial break, and her ears popped, releasing pressure from the inside of her head. It helped, and she straightened against the pillows, scooting up a little higher. Her eyes went back to the screen as the newscaster came on with local news.

"A young female truck driver was injured early this morning as a stolen truck crashed head-on into her empty rig as she crossed Stover Mountain. April Hayden, of Sacramento, suffered a concussion when her head struck the steering wheel. Doctors say it has resulted in a mild form of amnesia so that she remembers only fragments of what has happened and doesn't recall her name or where she was going when the truck hit."

Fascinated, she stared at the man making the comments. He was talking about her, but it sounded like a stranger he was describing. And as she watched, an inset picture of a young woman and a small wirehaired terrier was flashed on the TV screen. She leaned forward a little. The woman was laughing, her cheek nestled against that of the dog. It was Brush; she didn't know the young woman.

How can I not know her if it's me? Shaking her head, she examined the picture, trying to see herself as she must look to other people.

The announcer continued his report. "A small dog in the truck with Miss Hayden was not injured and is being cared for by one of the policemen who was chasing the stolen vehicle. Doctors say Miss Hayden will be released shortly."

Released? Where will I go? She gave her attention back to the report.

"The man driving the truck allegedly stole the vehicle after he'd robbed a convenience store in Red Bluff. He was hospitalized with a broken leg. Police have charged him with driving a stolen vehicle, driving without a license and possession of stolen goods."

The news went off, and a game show came on as April lay back on the pillows. An hour later her doctor came by. With gentle hands, he probed around her eyes, removing the small protective bandage he'd left there.

"I'm going to leave those stitches in for a few more days, April, or the lid might droop. If you're released Monday—and I reserve the option to not do so, you understand—I want you to see a doctor about Thursday to have the stitches removed."

"Suppose I still don't know who I am?"

He picked up her wrist and glanced at his watch. "If you have no dizziness or nausea, we may as well let you out. It might be one day—or a month—before you regain your memory."

"Or longer?"

"Or longer," he admitted.

He left her to ponder over that. She felt good—no headache, no nausea, no dizziness. In the quiet of the evening the only people she saw were visitors to other patients; she guessed no one knew her, so she shouldn't expect anyone.

But she watched the door until the nurse came by with a pill, and sleep came soon thereafter.

"IT'S SUNDAY," the nurse said in answer to her question. "How do you feel?"

"Sort of like I'm living in a vacuum," April told her. "I can't get used to knowing part of what's going on with all the gaps that are so important."

"You'll never get used to it. Hopefully, the blank spaces will disappear very quickly. I've seen it happen just in the blink of an eye."

"I've tried that," April assured her. "Nothing happened."

The girl laughed. "That's not exactly what I meant."

Nurses came and went. Meals were served. The doctor came by late that evening and told her he was going to release her on Monday morning.

April spent her time puzzling over her circumstances but gave up when she could find no answers in the blank spaces of her memory.

"Miss Hayden?"

She turned to see the two policemen who had rescued her from the accident—friendly faces belonging to people who were caring for Brush. She smiled. "Hello."

"We checked the addresses on the card over the visor in your rig," one of the men said. "Does the name Elsa Maxwell ring a bell?:

Slowly, she shook her head. "Who is she?"

"She manages Maxwell's Truck Stop in Sacramento where you store your rig and eat a good many meals during the week. She says she's known you for over three years."

Closing her eyes, she tried to bring an image of an Elsa she should know. She couldn't.

"Don't force yourself," the other man said. "She says you have no family."

"Well, I guess that's good," she conceded doubtfully. "At least no one's worried about my not coming home. Except Brush."

He laughed. "Brush is having a ball with my two boys. Of course you'll never be able to manage him again when they get through spoiling him."

"Where's my rig?"

"In the confiscated-vehicle lot at the police station. There's only a long scratch on the paint and a bent rim you'll probably have to replace."

"I was very lucky."

Both men nodded in agreement. "As soon as you're released, come on down and we'll get your signature on some papers. That's all you need to get your rig out of hock."

RUSS SPENT a good part of Sunday morning looking through the local papers for an item about April and found a small story on the front page of the third section that told him she was to be released soon.

He'd spent the night worrying about April, and he made it a point to be at Maxwell's Truck Stop early Monday to talk to Elsa. He was there when Wade Outen stopped by to say he was going through Red Bluff on his way north. It was only natural that Wade invite Russ to go along and keep April company on her way back to Sacramento when she was released from the hospital.

As they rode north in Wade's eighteen wheeler, Russ's thoughts were only of April and how badly she was hurt, but Wade wanted to talk about the April he knew.

"I've known April two years or more," he said. "She never mentioned any family. As a matter of fact, she told me her parents died several years ago and she was an only child."

"Yes," Russ told him. "They lived next door to my parents for years until their death."

Wade turned his way a moment and grinned a little. "I've been trying to get April to date me, but she won't. I accused her of having a boyfriend hidden away on the other side of the mountains. Told her he'd never be true to her as much as she's on the road."

Russ watched the other man, older than he was by a couple of years, he'd guess. Not bad-looking, with an easy way of talking, and friendly.

"What did she say to that?"

"Nothing. Just laughed. April doesn't care what I say. Or anyone else for that matter; she's the same with anybody. Goes shopping occasionally with Elsa and Katie, but that's all she does." He stared thoughtfully ahead at the highway. "I hope they're right when they say she isn't badly hurt. April's sorta special to me.''

April's very special to me, Russ wanted to tell him, but he remained silent as the miles rolled by.

Chapter Four

Russ followed the doctor down the hall, his long legs feeling the jar of each step. Stiff tension across his shoulders spread through his body as they neared the room where he knew he'd see April again. After six years he was going to see the woman who was once his wife.

The nightmares came back the night before, and he'd awakened sweating, reaching for April, as he'd done so many times, wanting to hold her, wanting reassurance that the days and nights of terror were over and he was back in civilization.

The world of kidnappers and terrorists was so far from civilization that he sometimes thought he'd have to have rehabilitation. His mind needed to be reprogrammed to adjust from total darkness to the light of day.

Seeing April should convince him that he was once more in a civilized world. He took a deep breath, aware of cold sweat in his armpits, and his mouth was so dry he couldn't swallow at all.

Standing just behind Dr. Wall as he spoke to April, Russ took advantage of their greetings to feast his eyes on the young woman who turned a quizzical gaze to them. He could almost feel the questions in her as she concentrated on Dr. Wall, with only a friendly glance at him.

His hungry gaze was busy, staring at the slender figure outlined beneath the bright white of hospital sheets. Russ remembered a more rounded body, fuller cheeks and brown hair without the strands of gray clearly visible in the thickness.

She's twenty-seven, and I remember twenty-one, he thought now. *I expected her to be the same woman-child I left behind. She isn't; not by any stretch of the imagination.*

As Dr. Wall checked her, April said, "I thought you'd forgotten me."

The doctor concentrated on her expression as he introduced the younger man. "This is Russell Calloway, April," he said, his fingers resting on her pulse.

She nodded to Russ, but her attention returned immediately to the doctor, surprising a waiting look on his face.

"I'm all right?" she asked, uneasiness in her voice.

"Yes, you're fine. The eye is healing very well. As soon as you remember April Hayden, you'll be back to normal." He turned toward Russ. "Mr. Calloway came up from Sacramento to drive back with you. He has known you—your, uh, family a long time."

"Oh." When she looked back at Russ, her look was full of concentrated attention, trying to recognize a family friend from long ago. She didn't. "That's very kind of you," she said. "I hope you don't have to miss work for this."

He shook his head and was surprised at the quietness of his voice when he answered. "No. I'm off for a few days. No trouble at all."

Dr. Wall, intent on any sign of recognition in April, told her, "Have your doctor get in touch with me, April. I'd like to hear how things work out for you."

"Yes, Dr. Wall. Thank you."

At the desk, Russ stood by as April signed release papers. Finished, they walked out into the crisp morning air, and she looked up at him.

"My rig's at the police lot. The nurse called a cab for us."

"How long have you been driving the rig?" he asked.

She shook her head. "I don't really know. A Mrs. Maxwell from Sacramento says she's known me over three years, so I assume I've driven at least that long." She shrugged. "I just hope I know how to drive it when I get in it."

A ghost of a smile touched his mouth. "I'll drive it for you. I'm sure I haven't forgotten how."

Their conversation was halted by the arrival of the cab, and a few minutes later they were dropped in front of the police station. Inside she asked for Patrolman Fountain.

The officer she had approached turned to yell, "Hey, Gil. Someone to see you."

He was grinning as he came from the adjoining room, and behind him trotted Brush. With a yip Brush was up in her arms before she reached for him.

"Must be yours," the man beside her said.

She grinned and turned to the policeman. "Thanks for keeping him. I hope he wasn't too much of a pest." Brush washed her face with a rough tongue, his small, hard body shivering with happiness at finding his mistress. She squeezed him lightly, stroking his wiry fur to reassure him that even though she remembered little else, she certainly knew who he was.

With a feeling close to what she termed miraculous, she sighed with relief. Everything's going to be all right, she decided.

"My boys didn't want to give him up." He walked behind a desk and reached to pick up a set of keys. "I'll show you where your truck is."

She put Brush down, and they followed the patrolman outside, Russell Calloway alongside them. Looking up, she saw the familiar lines of her rig. Down the driver's side was a wide slash of silver metal showing where the stolen truck had taken her paint with it. The rear wheel was bent only a little. She could make it to Sacramento with no trouble.

"Do you want me to drive?" Russell Calloway asked her.

"No. Let me see if I remember what I'm supposed to do," she said, climbing into the cab and letting Brush in beside her. She waved to Patrolman Fountain and started the motor. Russ swung up beside her.

Nothing was strange to her. The gears were familiar; every action she made came automatically, without her having to think about it. She frowned, shaking her head.

"I just don't understand partial amnesia. I could accept it if I didn't remember anything, but splotchy amnesia seems rather weird." She grinned at the man watching her. "Don't you think so?"

He continued to look at her, light blue eyes taking in her features one by one, finally settling on her mouth, which was still smiling.

"I understand any type of amnesia is baffling. But like you, I've never heard of sectional amnesia."

"Sectional? I like that description even better." She turned her attention to driving the vehicle, and they didn't talk for a while.

"Tell me about my family, Mr. Calloway," she said as they reached a cruising speed outside the city limits.

"I think I'd rather you called me Russ." He seemed to relax a little as he went on. "Your parents have been dead for at least seven or eight years. You were an only child."

She frowned. "Where do I live?"

"I only know what Mrs. Maxwell told me. I've been away for several years and have just got back into town to visit my folks. Mrs. Maxwell said you have an apartment but spend a lot of time on the road."

She chewed on the corner of her lower lip, frowning at the blankness she met at every corner. After long minutes of silence she gave a small shrug. "Dr. Wall said it could be tomorrow or next month." She took a deep breath. "Even next year. I hope I'm the type of person with lots of patience." She threw him a quick grin and looked back at the highway stretching in front of them.

Between them Brush lay still, content now with his head on April's leg. She let her right hand drop from the wheel to rub behind his stubby ears.

"Too bad Brush can't talk," she said.

"How long have you had him?" Russ asked.

She thought about it. "A long time. For years, I'm sure."

"I'm sorry. I keep asking these questions, forgetting you don't know any answers yet."

Something in his voice made her look at him to meet the direct gaze that seemed to see deep within her. A strange feeling like the glow of a firefly in a dark night flickered for a moment as their eyes met.

He looked sad, she thought. His eyes looked old even though he was probably not many years older than she.

Turning her attention back to the road, she hesitated, trying to analyze the feeling before she answered him. She couldn't. Odd was the only word she could associate with the fleeting awareness between them.

"Perhaps one question you ask will bring about a response, so feel free to ask. I sure would like to have some answers. I feel fine; that's what seems so peculiar."

"From the description on the newscast I'd say you were very fortunate."

She nodded. "I remember that much." She patted the dog beside her. "Brush warned me, but I was thinking of something else, I guess, and didn't pay much attention."

"How? How did he warn you?"

"By whining. He never whines. But he sat up in the seat and put his paw on my arm and whined. I thought he wanted out of the truck. He didn't; he wanted me out. I promised to stop at the next turnoff, but we never made it." She looked at him. "Strange. Really strange."

Russ laughed, a sound that made her glance his way again. Somewhere inside she decided she liked the way he laughed. It had a pleasant sound, like a fond old memory from an unremembered past.

"Next you'll be telling me your dog is psychic," he said.

She laughed, too. "Well, he is special. Maybe not psychic but special." She rubbed over her eye, letting her fingers skim over the tender cut.

"Do you feel okay?" he asked.

"Yes." They had reached the outskirts of Sacramento. "Can I drop you somewhere, Russ? I don't want to put you to any more trouble."

"Do you know how to get to the truck stop?"

She stopped at a light. "Yes, of course," she said, then turned to look at him in surprise. "I don't know how, but I do."

They stared at each other, and she was aware of the odd breathless feeling she had once before. "Doesn't that beat all?"

The light changed, and she pulled away, shaking her head. She might as well stop trying to figure out her sometimes-blank mind and wait until it cleared of its own accord.

"My car's at the truck stop," he said. "I got a ride as far as Red Bluff with a trucker who knew you. Name of Wade Outen."

She frowned. "How well does he know me?"

"Not as well as he'd like."

"Why do you say that?" she asked, giving him a quick glance.

"He told me he's been trying to get you to date him for some time." His voice was even, but there seemed to be a question along with the statement.

"Really? I don't remember." She caught her lower lip between her teeth in the move that was familiar to the man beside her. She concentrated on turning the rig from the interstate into a side street and a few moments later pulled into the fenced-in back lot at Maxwell's Truck Stop.

He waited as she reached under the dash and took out her logbook, making entries quickly. Marking a big asterisk near the entry, she wrote at the bottom of the page: Accident Report.

She picked Brush up from the seat and slid out the side, standing to look at the scarred paint on the door and the bent wheel. Russ came around the truck to look, running his hand along the roughness. He stooped to look at the wheel, pulling at the heavy spokes.

"I don't believe there's any damage to the wheel itself, but you'd better have it checked before your next trip." He stood up and turned to her. "When are you scheduled to make another run?"

"I don't know. I thought perhaps there might be a schedule in the café."

They walked side by side into the truck stop, and several people looked around at them. Behind the counter stood a blond-haired woman, a little on the heavy side.

"April!" she shouted, and raced around the counter faster than most small people would move. She stopped with her hands out toward April but didn't touch her.

Her voice was a loud whisper. "Are you okay?"

She nodded. "Are you Elsa?"

The color drained from the woman's face. "Oh, my God, they were telling the truth. You don't even know me."

April smiled uncertainly, giving a sidelong glance at Russ standing beside her. "I—I'm sorry." She shook her head. "I don't know anyone, it seems."

With visible effort, Else controlled her expression. "Come sit down. Maybe if we talk awhile, it might help." She waved toward a table where two men sat. "Don Roman, Pete Noonan."

The men nodded and said together, "Hi, April."

She swallowed, hoping her smile wasn't as stiff as it felt over her lips. The men were total strangers, as Elsa had been. "How are you?" she finally managed. A hand touched her arm, and she looked up at Russ uncertainly. He smiled and nodded, guiding her to the counter where Elsa was waiting.

They talked a long time. Elsa gave her a rundown of her usual work habits, including a schedule, posted along with others, on a bulletin board.

"When you take a trip, you pick up your next run from your delivery point. All are regular customers, so you won't have any trouble. I'm sure everyone saw the television reports." She leaned heavy arms on the counter.

"Did you see the one that had the picture of you and Brush?" she asked April.

She nodded, smiling. "I recognized Brush, anyway."

"That's the one I saw to know who she was, too," Russ commented.

"Wade Outen took that picture just a couple weeks ago."

"Wade Outen?" She turned to Russ. "You said—"

Russ nodded. "He's the one I rode with up to Red Bluff."

"He's sort of sweet on April," Elsa told them, smiling.

"We date?" April asked.

Elsa shook her head. "You never date anyone around here." She laughed, her generous flesh shaking a little with the movement. "Smart girl."

"I'm not sure about that. If I had dated him a lot, maybe he could help me remember something." She sipped at the coffee Elsa had placed in front of them, giving her cream to go in it, so it was an automatic action. April Hayden used cream in her coffee. Such a minor thing, but somehow it helped just knowing it was one of her habits.

"You weren't hurt bad physically, and we have that to be thankful for," Elsa said. She touched her arm. "It'll work itself out." She moved away to help a customer.

April let her gaze wander over the posters and calendars on the wall behind the counter, a big West-clox, a big head of deer antlers, an old Coca-Cola advertisement, a box of Almond Joy candy bars.

"I like Almond Joys," she said suddenly, and beside her, she felt Russ stiffen. She turned to him, smiling, but he was staring into his coffee cup, both hands almost hiding it.

He took a deep breath before he lifted his head to return her smile. The tight look around his mouth had deepened, and for a moment his eyes held a haunted look. The stirring in her chest prompted the vague questioning feelings that had surfaced several times as she talked to Russ.

She took a drink of the now-cool coffee, wondering. Russ Calloway was just home from someplace far away, he indicated. There was no ring on his left hand. Was he married?

What an odd thought, April Hayden. What possible difference could that make? He said he was a friend of the family—a long-ago friend. That's why you sense you've known him before. But that wasn't what caused the fluttering sensation in her chest. It was a heightened awareness of something between them.

Silly girl, her thoughts went on. *Just because he traveled a hundred miles to ride home with you—his civic duty. Maybe his mother told him it would be nice to help out a former family friend.*

Elsa was down the counter, talking to other customers, and she reached into her pocket for change to pay for her coffee, sliding off the stool as she did so.

"I have it, April," Russ said, and placed a bill next to their cups. "Where to now?"

"I'm going home," she said, and stopped. Her voice was hesitant as she continued. "Yes, I know where I live." She faced him. "I also know I have an old cream-colored car in the lot outside."

They stared at each other, and she shrugged, turning as Elsa came toward them. She smiled at the woman. "My schedule says Friday is my next run, so I have a couple days to recuperate. I have to see my doctor here before I go back on the road."

"Your doctor? I never knew you to be sick," Elsa said.

April thought a moment. "I have a dentist. Dr. Clint in the Arcade Plaza." Drawing a deep breath, she said, "Maybe I can get him to remove my stitches." When Elsa continued to look at her, she went on. "At any rate, I'm going home."

"Will you call me tonight before you go to bed?" Elsa asked.

"Why?"

"I'll worry if you don't," the woman said simply.

She grinned. "Okay."

It was midafternoon, and the sun coming from the west was warm if you stayed out of the brisk breeze.

It ruffled April's hair as she stood looking across the big lot where several rigs, including hers, were parked in marked areas.

Without a word, she started across the opposite side of the lot, glancing around to see that Brush was at her heels. She stooped to pick him up and looked at Russ.

"I can manage, Russ. You've done enough for me."

"I'll follow you home just to make sure. Your address was in your things."

"Oh, yes, I guess it would be." They walked in silence to her car, and she removed her keys from the shoulder bag that had been returned to her from her truck. Curious, she pulled out her billfold and opened it. The same picture of her and Brush smiled at her from the plastic inserts. There were no other pictures, only identification cards, driver's license and social security card.

"April Hayden doesn't have anyone, it would appear," she said, putting the billfold back into the bag and zipping it closed.

"Yes, it looks as though there's no immediate family," Russ said.

He opened the door of her car, and she slid into the seat, scooting Brush across to the passenger's side. He settled down immediately, curled into a ball as he waited for her to start the car. She relaxed a little as she watched him. He knew he was where he belonged, and perhaps, before long, she would remember everything that remained a puzzling blank to her.

"You don't have to—" she started to tell Russ when he interrupted her.

"I'm going with you, just to make sure you get there. I'll follow."

Without thinking about it, she made the few turns down four streets and pulled into a parking place at the side of a two-story clapboard building. The sparkling white of the outside was reflected inside as she went up the narrow stairs, Russ close behind her.

Her key fit instantly into the door with the letter "B" on it, and she let it swing inward as she took a step inside. It smelled slightly dusty, the way a room would if it had remained unused for a while.

It was a large room with a couch and big chair to one side, a coffee table, a lamp table with a radio on it and a small hassock. At one side there was an apartment-sized refrigerator and small range with cabinets over the counter. There was no table or kitchen chairs.

Sensing Russ behind her, she went into the room, watching Brush go immediately to a dish near the sink. She threw her handbag on the couch and followed him, picking up the dish to run fresh water into it and return it to the little dog, who drank thirstily.

Russ hadn't spoken, and she looked around at him. "Looks like April not only doesn't have any family or friends; she had little else besides."

He half turned away from her but not before she saw the expression on his face. He felt sorry for her!

She stiffened, then said lightly, "I don't need much room if I'm gone all the time." *Now why in the world am I making excuses to him,* she wondered. *He doesn't care what I do or don't do, what I have or don't have.* She wished he'd leave to let her collect her thoughts; collect herself even from the peculiar sensation of living on a foreign planet that she once visited enough to have vague recollections about it. Nothing solid; only vague.

He seemed to sense her feelings. "If you think you'll be all right, April, I'll leave now. Only if you think you're okay."

She nodded. "I'm fine, Russ. Thanks for everything." She followed him to the door and looked up as he paused.

"I'll call you later," he promised.

"Thank you," she said, standing there to listen to the click of the door closing, his footsteps moving down the hall to the stairway. She heard his car door open and close, the motor start, and as he pulled into the street, the diminishing sound of the tires on the pavement. Turning, she faced Brush, who sat in the middle of the room, stubby tail thumping.

"Well, Brush, fill me in on what's happened up till now." She laughed at the happy expression on the small dog's face and bent to scoop him into her arms before she sat on the comfortable old couch and looked around the strange but familiar room.

"You know something, Brush?" she asked the small dog. "I think the word 'strange' will become the most common expression in my vocabulary unless I find out who April Hayden is pretty soon."

Brush jumped on the couch, turned around twice and lay down with his head on her lap. He knew April whether she did or not.

A BLOCK AWAY from April's apartment, Russ pulled to the curb and stopped, leaning his head on his arms crossed over the steering wheel. The old cream-colored car April drove was the one his parents gave them the down payment for as a wedding gift. How many times he'd seen April chew on her lip trying to adjust their limited budget to stretch for a payment on the car.

April rode the bus to school while he drove the car, because his part-time job was farther away than hers. When he left her, he'd left the car, maybe because of his guilt feelings, but he liked to think that for once he'd done something to make things a bit easier for her.

He straightened over the wheel. April was no longer the young girl he'd left six years ago; she was a lovely woman, her face serene and content, even not knowing much about herself. She was happy, evidently feeling no loss because Russ was no longer her husband.

And Russ? Well, Russell Calloway still loved April Hayden.

Chapter Five

It took only a few minutes the next morning to learn that April Hayden kept little of any consequence in the plain one-room apartment. A small jar of peanut butter, a jar of instant coffee and a plastic-wrapped package of Almond Joy candy bars were the only items in the cabinet over the sink.

The refrigerator held a jar of powdered milk substitute—for coffee, she guessed. April didn't stay around the apartment enough to stock groceries, she decided.

A closet near the bathroom held a few dresses, coveralls, jeans and a coat. Boots, sneakers and a pair of black sandals made up her footwear. Driving gloves lay on a shelf along with a white cowboy hat.

I'm a good guy, she thought. *I wear a white hat.*

The tiny bathroom had a shelf for linens that held enough bedclothes to change and several sets of towels with matching washcloths. The medicine chest above the sink held a few cosmetics and a bottle of aspirins. That was all.

She went back to sit on the couch with a cup of the instant coffee that tasted as she thought mud might taste.

"I'm either not too particular what my coffee tastes like, or I've forgotten how it's done," she said aloud.

Brush walked over to the door, glancing back to see if she was paying attention.

"I'm coming," she said, picking up her jacket and handbag. "Doesn't seem to be much to stay around here for."

As she locked the door behind her, she thought of Russ Calloway's phone call just before she went to sleep the night before. She had remembered to call Elsa, assuring her she was fine, telling her she'd be there for breakfast. But she had forgotten Russ said he would call.

"Do you have any headache now, April?" he asked after they exchanged greetings.

"No. I'm a little tired and achy, but I guess that's to be expected. Aside from the soreness just above my eye, no pain at all."

He talked on a few minutes longer and said goodnight. She was still thinking about him when sleep overtook her.

Now, as she stepped out into the late-winter morning, her thoughts returned to Russ Calloway. No particular reason; he was just there. The craggy features gave him an older look, or maybe it was the almost-haunted look in his eyes that gave the impression of being old.

The thick brown hair had a lot of gray in it, but then, so did hers. At the thought of the streaks through the deep brown of her hair, her hand went up to brush it away from her cheek as the breeze swept it around.

"I should wear my cowboy hat and hide the gray," she told Brush as he came skipping back from his sojourn to the side of the yard. "I'm really not old enough to have gray hair; wonder if I've had a hard life?" she mused out loud, and found herself wondering how she just *knew* she was twenty-seven years old.

Other facts teased at her senses as she drove the short distance to the truck stop. She sat in the car several minutes, taking in the somehow-familiar sight of trailer rigs parked since last night and those that had pulled in that morning, the diesel engines idling. Mentally, she identified the trucks and the companies they represented.

How, she wondered. *How can I remember those unknown companies and not remember April Hayden? Trying too hard,* she decided, then patted Brush's wiry coat and slid out of the car, walking with her head down into the building.

Inside, she glanced around, seeing not a familiar face in the ones who looked up at her to smile and call greetings. She answered them and went to the counter. Elsa turned around and saw her.

"April?" She hesitated only a moment. "The usual?" she asked.

Startled, April opened her mouth, then grinned. "Sure. Why not?"

The coffee Elsa poured for her was a vast improvement over the instant she had made for herself earlier. Curiously, she waited to see what her "usual" would be. It wasn't long before she saw. It was one fluffy buttermilk pancake, a patty of sausage and one egg, over medium. She tasted it. It was just as good as she didn't remember it would be.

"Good morning, April."

Looking around at the quiet voice beside her, she met Russell Calloway's smile. A cautious smile, she thought. *Now why is he being cautious with me? I have no designs on him.* A flicker of a strange sensation in her stomach almost denied that.

He sat beside her, his eyes taking in the food on her plate. Before he turned to greet Elsa, she saw the tightening of his mouth, and he sort of flinched away from her.

Looking back at her plate, the only thing she saw that might make him look away was the amount there. *It isn't all that much,* April thought in surprise as she remembered the movement of his shoulders. *Maybe I'm still a growing girl.* She glanced down at her slim figure, no bulges showing in the jeans and flannel shirt she wore.

Halfway listening to what he ordered, she went on eating, smiling at Elsa as she refilled her coffee cup. As she turned away, her eyes met those of Russ in the mirror over the counter. After a fleeting moment, she looked back at her plate.

"Still sore?" he asked after a few moments.

She shook her head. "Except for a few spots I touch unexpectedly now and then. The eye, of course, but it doesn't hurt."

"How about Brush? Any aftereffects?"

"He's fine. Just like we never left the apartment."

He seemed to stiffen beside her but didn't make any comment until after his plate was put in front of him. "Brush doesn't have much place to run there, does he?"

Frowning, she glanced at him. "If I'm gone all the time, perhaps he gets a chance to run along my routes." Her voice hinted that she thought it was none of his business.

He opened his mouth to speak, met her direct look and clamped his lips together, turning away from her. They sat in silence until she finished her breakfast, slipped from the stool and paid her ticket. Nodding to everyone in general, she headed for the door, noticing in spite of herself the stiffness in Russ Calloway's back.

"Take care, April," Elsa said as she was leaving. It sounded as if she had heard the words before, and she waved her good-bye, going outside to stand for a moment, trying to bring into focus the fragmented memories hanging around the edge of her consciousness. She shook her head; no good—no good at all.

There was no reason to return to the single room she undoubtedly called home, so she turned her car onto Interstate 5, heading south. She remembered the suburban areas she drove through, and when the highway intersected Interstate 80, she turned west, then back north to make the circle around the city complete as she came back to Interstate 5. Restless, she drove back into the business section and parked.

If it's Wednesday, this must be Sacramento, she mused. On the seat beside her, Brush awoke and stretched, moving a little closer to her before he lay down again. Absently, her hand stroked the little dog, and he sighed contentedly.

She rolled the glass down enough to give Brush air, got out and locked the door behind her, strolling along with the morning work force. Hands deep in the pockets of her jacket, she walked, thinking: an accident she couldn't avoid, a lapse in memory, the meeting with an old family acquaintance, questions that no one could answer, a feeling that there was more to Russ Calloway than she could see. Or maybe it was only a feeling April Hayden had for Russ Calloway.

Wade Outen. *I'll talk to him when he comes off the road,* she thought, stopping to look into a window. Elsa said— She couldn't remember exactly what it was Elsa said about Wade. She must not have really dated him but knew him from the truck stop and their schedules, which crisscrossed now and then.

At the newsstand she picked up the morning paper, taking a copy of the San Francisco paper along with the local one. She rolled them up, tucked them under her arm and returned to the car.

It was nearly noon when she and Brush found their way to the apartment. She went to put water on for coffee, wrinkling her nose at the prospect of drinking a cup like the one she made that morning. Serving Brush fresh water and a milkbone from a package on the counter, she finally sat down with her paper.

The front section yielded the usual catastrophes, outrageous utility rate requests, unpredictable weather and the like. She turned to the local section and stared at Russ Calloway's picture. Her heart righted itself from the flip it took as she read the caption: "Russ Calloway, Former Hostage, to be Honored."

It took several seconds for her to remember that she had seen the TV program showing the safe return of two men based somewhere overseas, men who had been taken hostage by terrorists and only returned when a huge sum of money was paid by their company. Russ Calloway was one of those men.

Her gaze returned to his picture. It wasn't very clear, but it showed the strain she had seen in his face. That was what was bothering him—and no wonder. It must have been a traumatic experience.

But he had taken time out to come to check on her because at one time their families had been friends. How much family did he have? Was there a wife? The article mentioned nothing concerning relatives, but it had possibly been printed days ago, when she hadn't seen news or a paper.

The honor was a dinner and recognition of his service in the local chapter of the Veterans of Foreign Wars. He was evidently well thought of in the area, and the hometown folks were letting him know it. He looked unhappy and very tired

Thoughtful, she went to get her coffee. Unhappily, it was just as bad as her first cup of the day.

With feet propped up, she finished reading both papers, then stared at the ceiling. "What in the world do I do with myself the days I don't have a schedule to meet?" she asked the sleeping Brush. "You certainly aren't any entertainment." She watched him for a moment, rousted him off the couch and opened it up to make her bed. At two o'clock in the afternoon, she undressed, pulled on her flannel robe and crawled beneath the warm blankets. In minutes she was asleep.

SHE AWAKENED the next morning with a groggy headache, surely from sleeping so much. She woke up at eight the night before, got up, fed Brush, ate a candy bar and was back in bed at ten, thinking she'd spend the rest of the night tossing and turning. She had gone to sleep immediately.

A dose of caffeine will help me, she thought. *Not mine,* she amended, and with her body protesting, she dressed and headed for Elsa's.

It was a particularly busy morning for Elsa, and they did little more than exchange pleasantries as the truckers were taken care of and sent on their way. She sat in a booth near the back, watching the heavy breakfast traffic.

"Aren't you supposed to see the doctor today?"

She looked up at Elsa and smiled. "I still don't know who to see unless you have a recommendation."

Elsa slid her solid form into the booth opposite her. "Call the medical clinic down the street here and see if they'll give you a doctor's name, one who'll see you right away." She looked April over before she went on. "That cut is healing good, but you definitely should see a doctor before you go back on the road."

"Yes, I know," April said. "My insurance company would frown at my not doing that. I have to send in a medical report for them to pay me."

"Have you seen Russ?"

Startled, she looked up. "Not since yesterday when he came in to eat breakfast."

"He didn't call you last night?"

"No. Why would you think he'd call me?"

Elsa shrugged, then grinned. "He seemed interested."

"Well, he is an old family friend," she said.

The older woman leaned forward. "You don't for one moment believe that, do you?"

"Yes, of course. Why else would he drive all the way to Red Bluff to check on someone involved in an accident if he didn't know me from somewhere?"

Elsa frowned. "I'm still trying to figure it out." She hesitated, then went on, "You know he's just back from Egypt where he was held hostage by terrorists, don't you?"

Nodding, April said, "Yes. He looks very sad, don't you think? Like something's making him very unhappy. There's probably more to the kidnapping story than we've heard."

"You're right. You know the newspapers and the big companies are in cahoots to fool the public. We may never know the real story behind the headlines."

Elsa got up to serve a customer and a few minutes later came back to stand by April. "What I really wanted to know is if you actually feel able to fill your schedule you're posted for tomorrow? Wade's between runs; I'm sure he'd do it for you."

"Wade's the one who's quote sweet on April unquote?" she asked. "No, thanks. All I need is to be obligated to Wade, not even knowing why I never agreed to go out with him." She laughed, adding, "I feel completely capable of taking the run. It's only to Redding."

"I have to take care of this place, April, but promise me you'll see a doctor before you leave and let me know what he says," Elsa said as she left her.

She promised, watching the woman move across the wide room. Elsa had looked out for her and was probably her best friend, if the truth were known. She would certainly keep her informed.

Finishing the breakfast, she paid, leaving by the side door to reach her car. It was chilly, and she turned up the collar of her jacket, shivering as she slid behind the wheel. Brush stood up to sniff at her, then lay back down.

"Dog's life," she said. "I should be so lucky."

At the medical center Elsa mentioned she told the receptionist her story and received a number to wait for a doctor to call her. She settled down with a three-

month-old magazine and was just getting interested in
the story when her name was called.

"Dr. Sarter will see you, Miss Hayden. Room 302,
down the hall to your left. Just knock and enter."

Following the hall in the direction the girl pointed,
she found the room and knocked, pushing the door
open when invited to do so. She faced a bearded man
in a white coat, frowning at the card in his hand.

Still frowning, he looked at her. "You were in an
accident and have no memory of who you are, Miss
Hayden?"

"Well..." At her hesitation he lifted his brows and
waited. "I remember bits and pieces."

"What type bits and pieces?"

"Almost anything but who I am. I remember the
accident. I remembered I had a little dog, how to get
places, that I owned a truck and did intrastate hauling, where I lived, even how old I am."

The doctor watched her steadily as she went on. "I
just don't remember April Hayden," she finished.

"Sit up here and let me take a look at that eye," he
told her, indicating the sheet-covered narrow bed.

He examined the eye, shining a bright penlight into
both eyes, turning it away to flash it back several
times.

"Any headaches?"

"Not since Monday."

"Does your vision blur? Do you occasionally see
double?"

"No."

"Who stitched up the eye?"

"Dr. Wall in Red Bluff."

He nodded. "Nice, neat job. No fractures?"

"He said I had a slight concussion which would account for the partial amnesia." What had Russ called it: sectional. Now why should she think of Russ Calloway?

"Let's take an X ray to be on the safe side, April. I suppose Dr. Wall told you this was a common thing with amnesia and that you could remember at any time?"

"Yes."

He handed her a white smock, pointing behind a curtain. "I'll send the technician to get those pictures, and I'll see you back in here."

The technician came in, smiled a professional smile at her, gave her directions to turn her head several different ways and said, "That's all," then disappeared.

"Sit here and I'll snip those stitches," Dr. Sarter told her, suiting words to action as she sat still. He dropped the thin pieces of thread into the wastebasket and pressed his fingers gently along the scar at the edge of her eyebrow.

"If you don't have trouble with this popping open, I won't need to see you unless something shows in the X ray. Make an appointment to see us in three months for a follow-up." He smiled as she got up to leave. "Maybe when you come back, you can tell us who April Hayden is."

"I'll call you if I find out before the three months are up," she promised. At the reception desk she was told to call two weeks ahead for the appointment. Promising to do just that, she walked out into a blowy afternoon and went home.

Chapter Six

The mechanic had replaced the damaged rim of the wheel on her rig and checked the oversized tire to make sure it was in good shape. She had an appointment to have the side painted the following week. Nodding her head in approval and satisfaction, she headed toward Redding.

Once on the open highway, she pulled her John Deere cap over her thick hair, rolled the window down a bit for fresh air and settled back to enjoy the ride. Beside her, Brush was already curled into a tight ball, sleeping away.

Her smile at the small animal was indulgent. *Perhaps you've the right idea, Brush. Sleep, as long as you have pleasant dreams.* She frowned. She couldn't recall dreaming at all.

Hmm. I wonder if April Hayden ever dreamed?

Dr. Sarter hadn't been much help in relieving her questions, but he evidently didn't think there was any danger in her condition—aside from the uncertainty, of course.

When she related the doctor's evaluation to Elsa, the woman who seemed to appoint herself as her pseudomother wasn't too happy with the results.

"He couldn't give you any indication whether you'd regain your memory—if ever?"

"Well, no," April told her. "Like I said, he took out the stitches; I'm fine except—"

"When do you have to go back to him?"

"He took X rays, and if he finds anything spectacular, he'll call me. Otherwise, I go back in three months."

As April thought about Elsa and all her motherly clucking over her, she grinned. *She's going to worry about me whether I need it or not.*

Her thoughts went on over the morning's happenings, and her pulse speeded up as she thought of Russ. He'd come in just before she finished her breakfast.

"Are you going on a trip?" he asked, his tone registering disapproval.

"Yeah. Just up to Redding. I'll be back tonight."

"Are you up to it?"

"Dr. Sarter says I'm fine, aside from not knowing very much." She gave him a grin. "Maybe I'm better off for not knowing who I am."

The firm lips she was watching as she spoke tightened, leaving a white line around his wide mouth. A muscle jerked in his cheek, and she stared in surprise at the change in his expression.

"He's probably right. A lot of us could do with some blanks in our memories." He spoke abruptly, his voice cold.

"I didn't mean—" She'd hesitated then, trying to think what she'd said to account for the coolness. Perhaps something reminded him of his recent experience with the terrorists. Rummaging around in her mind for a way to get away from a delicate conversation, she was startled by his next question.

"May I call you tonight?" It was a stiff, formal question.

She didn't date anyone, Elsa had told her. There would be no repercussions from a jealous boyfriend if she agreed to go out with Russ. She wanted to go.

"Yes," she finally told him. "I'll be home after four o'clock."

Running their short conversation over in her mind, she felt an uplift to her spirits at the thought of seeing Russ again so soon. She gave her attention once more to the trip ahead of her, recognizing every hill and curve between Sacramento and Redding, just as though she'd been on that road many times—which she had, of course.

The trip was uneventful; she delivered her merchandise at the lumberyard in Redding, having no trouble finding it, no trouble with manifests. The puzzle that was April Hayden continued to exist without anyone working it out. The people at her destination knew her, knew about the accident, questioned her about it, teased and warned her to be careful.

It wasn't quite four o'clock when she unlocked the door of the old car, wondering idly why she bothered to lock it. It was so old that if anyone stole it, they'd be doing her a favor. Brush hopped into the front seat, and she slid in beside him. Driving the short distance to her apartment, she pondered over the bankbook she'd found as she rummaged through her handbag. April Hayden was a thrifty soul. She could pay cash for a new car if she wanted to. The car she drove was several years old according to the registration, but it had low mileage and seemed to be in good running condition. Still, she wondered why April Hayden hung on to the old vehicle.

Sentimental value, she decided as she watched Brush scamper to his favorite grassy strip, then come racing back to run up the steps with her.

Inside the apartment, she shed her work uniform of jeans and flannel shirt and went to the closet. She laughed softly to herself as she surveyed the small choice of clothing she saw before her.

She was still standing there when the phone rang. By the way her heart misbehaved, she knew it was Russ before she picked it up.

Before he said anything, she heard his deep indrawn breath. "You did all right on the trip?" he asked.

"Sure. No problems. Everyone was helpful—except to tell me how to remember who I am."

His hesitation was certainly obvious, but when he spoke, his voice was even and interested only in her. "Did we decide where we were going for dinner?"

"You'd better decide, Russ. All I know is the truck-stop café."

He laughed, a deep, soothing sound. Her body responded with a delicious quiver. "Let's save Elsa's for breakfast. We'll find a good place according to your food preference. I'll pick you up at seven."

She sat there, wondering at her reactions to Russ. Despite not knowing him at all, she was getting some positive vibrations that caused questions sans answers. *Well,* she thought. *I'm full of questions no one can answer. Why do I worry about the ones that come up at the mention of his name?*

Back at her closet, she pushed the uninteresting items around, finally taking a long-sleeved dress down to lay across the back of the couch for inspection. It was charcoal-and-red plaid with a soft wide belt. A narrow stand-up collar of white closed at the throat with a string tie; the long sleeves fastened at the lacy white cuffs with tiny white buttons.

Glancing down at her slim body in skimpy panties and bra, she went looking for a slip, finding it in the small chest in the bathroom. She put the dress over her head and buttoned the front down to the full skirt, cinching the wide belt around her narrow waist. In the small mirror over the bathroom sink, she inspected the result. Not bad, she decided.

When Russ knocked on the door, she was ready. A touch of blush to her cheeks had brightened her otherwise-colorless appearance. A tiny outline of pale lipstick helped some. There wasn't much to be done to the thick brown hair except brush it back and let it lie there, gray streaks blatantly exposed.

Smiling, she stood aside to let him enter, noticing for the first time that he was quite tall and also thin. He could stand some good meals himself, she thought. *Perhaps he lives alone like me and doesn't eat right.* Suddenly, she remembered that she had never decided if he were married or not. Hopefully not, if he asked her out.

He was nodding as she looked up at him. "You look delightful, April," he said. He didn't sit down but stood near her, long arms hanging at his side. A glimpse of what he must have looked like as a young man intruded for an instant and was gone.

"What did you decide we'd eat?" he asked.

"I don't know. I'm hungry enough to eat anything," she told him without thinking.

He laughed, that soft laugh she was beginning to like. He didn't laugh often enough. "Okay. We'll take it from there."

"Be good," she told Brush as she checked the lock on the door. "Don't let any burglars run off with you; you're my most prized possession." She smiled at Russ, only to meet the expression she decided meant he was thinking of something not so pleasant. He still looked unhappy to her way of thinking. Perhaps it was the lines drawn deeply around his mouth.

It would be nice to smooth them away, she thought, and felt a curious thrill as she imagined touching his mouth. *Uh-oh,* she cautioned herself. *He's only taking you to dinner because he feels sorry for the April Hayden who doesn't really know that's who she is. Besides, he thinks I'm hungry and having a hard time making ends meet.*

The trucking business was quite profitable, if her bankbook was any indication, she wanted to tell him, but she somehow knew that he wouldn't appreciate that. She walked beside him out to the new-looking beige-and-brown sedan.

As he drove, she examined him: a brown sports coat with suede elbow patches, darker brown pants and white shirt open at his throat, no tie. Aside from the sternness of his craggy features, he was rather handsome. She smiled as he gave her a brief glance, catching her appraisal of him.

A fleeting expression darkened his eyes before he smiled back at her and said, "Let's try Gordon's Seafood Anchor."

She nodded, her interest centered on the wide mouth, deciding her stomach's satisfaction was being put behind her absorption with other things. For some reason she kept wondering how that mouth would feel on hers.

Perhaps it's been a long time since I was kissed, she thought, and a trickle of expectancy heightened the color in her cheeks.

The outside of the restaurant brought no familiar feelings to her as other buildings had done, and she theorized she had never been inside. It was quietly elegant in the old-fashioned decor of seagoing men. Anchors and nets hung on the walls. The lights were old sea lanterns, flickering just enough to allow them to see the tables, covered with heavy cream-colored linens.

"Would you like me to order, April, or do you remember a preference?" he asked as they looked over the menu.

"Please order for me," she said.

As the waitress returned, he gave orders she didn't pay much attention to. In this place, it must be good, if you could judge by the prices she glanced at. Russ was used to this type of dining, she guessed, noticing the ease with which he indicated the choices.

"April, do you st—" He stopped abruptly as she raised dark brown eyes filled with inquiring lights.

The April he knew preferred the light fruity taste in wines. He'd seen her spend half an hour reading labels on the least expensive bottles of Napa Valley wines, carefully selecting the best buy for their money. The times they could splurge had been few and far between during those years of marriage.

His successful career allowed him to pick rare and expensive wines from the finest European vineyards without regard for price. It had been a long time since he'd had to think about what he paid for anything he wanted at any given moment.

At that precise moment he'd have given anything to be able to take April in his arms and tell her she belonged to him. No—*once* she'd belonged to him. He swallowed painfully and started over. "They have an excellent white wine if you think you'd like to try it."

"Yes, I'd like that."

As the girl left, April looked curiously back at Russ, busying himself with unfolding the napkins across his knees, avoiding her eyes.

"Do you come here often?" she asked.

"I haven't been around much in the past few years," he said. "But when I'm in the area, I do come in here. It's the best for seafood."

She leaned her elbows un-Emily Post-like on the table. "Will you go back to Cairo to your job there?"

He shook his head. "I'll be going to Australia to the company headquarters based in Sydney."

A tightness in her chest interfered with her breathing. He was already on his way to another foreign country. The United States must not appeal to him.

She sat back and surveyed the man across from her. *I don't even know who he is and already I don't want him to go out of my life. How ridiculous. April Hayden, whoever you are, you're not too bright.*

"When will you be leaving?" she asked.

"I have a month's leave before I report."

The girl set glasses of wine in front of them, and April turned hers around, watching the few bubbles settle in the amber-colored liquid.

"To your health, April," Russ toasted her, his glass held toward her. "And may your memory, when it returns to you, bring you much happiness."

"Thank you," she said, and took a sip of the wine. It tasted of the rich fruity grapes the California valleys were famous for, and she ran the tip of her tongue over her lips, savoring it. Looking up at him, she surprised the pain in his eyes that she had seen more than once.

It was there in the darkening of the light blue color of his eyes, the tightening of his lips to emphasize the lines around his mouth, the jerky movement of his hands as he moved them beneath the table out of her sight.

She was curious about why he was a kidnap victim but didn't want to stir any more unpleasant memories. "Does your company have any offices in the United States?" Why don't you work here instead of foreign countries, she wanted to ask him.

"Oh, yes. They have offices in New York, Chicago, St. Louis, Houston."

"I hate to admit I don't know what ARCOT does. I don't even know what all those capital letters stand for." She smiled easily at her own ignorance.

To her surprise he laughed, and for a moment the pain disappeared as his eyes crinkled at the corners. "You'd never remember what the name is, anyway, April, but actually it translates to something like Allied Region of Cyanamid Overseas Terminals. Stateside offices simply go under the name of Allied Cyanamid."

"Chemicals?"

"Well, yes. The company is diversified. We have pharmaceutical laboratories, petroleum refineries, airplane-parts factories, gold mines, banks." He stopped as she stared at him, openmouthed.

"That hardly sounds like it would add up to ARCOT."

He grinned. "You never know what results you'll get from certain chemical formulas."

Their wineglasses were refilled, and Russ moved a small plate of cheeses closer to her. April was intent on how to phrase an interesting question.

"You're not married?" There, it was out. The question that had been nudging her since she met him—only a week ago? The accident seemed way in the past, or perhaps it was her busy mind searching for answers that seemed to take so long.

The quiet answer he gave her was disconcerting. "I'm divorced." It was a long time before he continued. "We were both very young—too young." He was watching her now, his gaze going over her face, lingering on her mouth, to her eyes, to her hair. He couldn't miss the gray with that concentrated attention.

"How long were you married?"

"A bit over three years."

Their food arrived and interrupted the conversation that was becoming very important to her. She wanted to know if the sadness in his face was because of the divorce. Did he still love his wife? He must be over thirty; he looked much older to her untrained eyes.

He changed the subject before she could pursue her line of questioning. "When is your next scheduled run, April?"

"Monday. I'm finally getting a southern trip. Just when the weather turns nice and the snows don't threaten me in the mountains, I get the southern jobs." She smiled across at him. "Brush will be happy because he likes the windows down so he can stick his head out."

"Where down south?"

"Bakersfield."

"What are you taking down there?"

"Farm equipment. Replacement parts for tractors, mostly." She put down her fork to take a sip of wine, wrinkling her nose as a bubble tickled it.

"How long is this trip?" He seemed to be holding his breath as he waited for her answer, his fork upraised over his plate.

"I'll be back late Tuesday," she said.

"Are most of your trips overnight ones?" he asked, seeming to relax a little as he went on eating.

"If I go to San Diego or north to Crescent City or to Aluras, I take a couple of days. Across the mountains I don't make as good time on the road as when I'm on all interstate."

He nodded, shifting his lanky body a little. "Whatever made you become a truck driver, April?"

When she didn't answer him right away, he raised his head to meet her smile. "I have no idea, Russ. If you knew my family well years ago, perhaps you remember what I was like as I was growing up. Was I a tomboy?"

The raw suffering was naked in his face for an instant, hidden from her as he put his napkin to his mouth and lowered his head so she could no longer see his expression.

"Are you okay?" she asked after a moment.

"Yes." He nodded for emphasis. "I must have swallowed too quickly." He sipped his wine. "Would you like a cup of coffee now?"

"No, thanks," she said.

He cleared his throat. "Yes, I remember you as a tomboy. Of course, that was a long time ago. I have no idea why April Hayden decided she'd like to drive a truck."

"For one thing, I don't think I'd like to work inside buildings all day. And the pay's quite good," she went on. "You don't like being inside, either, do you? Is your job as engineer outside most of the time."

He nodded. "Yes. A big percentage of the time."

"Would you like dessert?" the waitress interrupted them.

Russ looked at her, and she shook her head. "Definitely not."

He declined along with her and took the check from the girl, holding April's chair out so she could stand easily. She didn't turn to watch him, but she knew exactly how he looked. His long arms dangled at his sides; his head tilted downward to look at her; there were questions in his eyes and something else. A waiting look.

He seemed poised on the edge of committing himself to a statement, of demanding more answers from her that she couldn't give. Not that she didn't want to answer him; she just plain didn't know. She was April Hayden. He was Russ Calloway, a long-ago friend of the family who had somehow lost touch. And she had somehow lost a part of her life to an accident.

Chapter Seven

Russ glanced at his watch in the dashlights of the car as he pulled from the parking area of the restaurant.

"The circus is in town. Would you like to go?"

"Clowns and elephants and cotton candy?" she asked.

A slight smile touched his mouth. "Are you still hungry?"

She groaned. "Hardly," she denied, "but it sounds like the circus."

"Someone gave the tickets to my dad, and I stuck them in my pocket, if you're up to it."

"Sounds like fun. Where is it?"

"At the West Side Coliseum. You haven't read about it? It's been on all the television networks with posters all over town."

"I don't have a television set, although I watch the news at Elsa's. Probably watched at the wrong times. I haven't paid much attention to anything this week."

He gave her a quick look. "I guess it has been rather disturbing to find you're a stranger to yourself."

"It's very odd to look in the mirror and see what you look like and not know how to connect the face with a name or a personality. It's sort of like part of you is missing; you know it belongs there, but some-how you can't fit it in."

The glaring lights of the coliseum came at them as he turned the corner, and he had to concentrate to guide the car in the heavy traffic. Men with flash-lights motioned them into dusty lanes where they sat another five minutes before being signaled into a slot.

"Are we dressed for the circus?" she asked, look-ing down at her three-inch heels.

He laughed his comfortable laugh. "It isn't far. We were lucky to get to park this close."

Holding on to her arm, he guided her along with the crowd, and minutes later they were ushered into seats in the sixth row, back from the balustrade, giving them an outstanding view of the actions that would be in the arena.

"Who does Mr. Calloway know to rate tickets like this?" she asked over the noise of the crowd.

He shook his head. "I didn't ask. Just took them." He grinned at her, looking boyish for just a moment until the anguished look returned to his eyes even as she watched him.

She turned to look out over the crowd, a Saturday night crowd mixed with lots of children. Entertain-ment for kids and grown-ups alike. She must have, at one time, loved the circus, because she could feel the excitement building as starting time approached. She sat back to watch.

"Want some popcorn?" Russ asked beside her, and she nodded without turning. A moment later she ac-cepted the warm box, still watching the elephants being led into the ring. The tiny one cavorting behind the two huge beasts was already getting laughs from the crowd.

As the program got under way, with all acts involved, she became completely engrossed, forgetting the man sitting beside her. When intermission came, she was surprised to find her hand held closely in Russ's big one.

Turning, her eyes still wide from trying to see everything all at once, she found his head bent toward her, their faces almost touching.

He laughed, his free hand touching her cheek. "You look like you're twelve."

Tightening her fingers around his, she whispered, "In that case you should have gotten me in for half price."

And suddenly he wasn't smiling anymore. His eyes once more saw things she didn't, and he sat up away from her. She gave him a questioning look as he turned away and looked back at the arena where clowns were frolicking.

He's afraid I'm really strange, she thought. *He doesn't know what I'm hiding by refusing to remember who I am.* The thought hit her with a surprising thump in her chest.

Russ neither saw the action in the arena nor thought that the woman beside him was strange. If anything, he was the one who was different, changed from the young man at one time married to April. He felt her warmth through their entwined fingers as her thumb moved back and forth over the knuckle of his forefinger. He wanted to squeeze tightly, hold on to keep from losing the familiar feel of April's skin against his.

Without warning, he remembered the day he filed for divorce. A piece of paper that would give him his final freedom from April and a marriage that started too soon. Until then he'd been busy, finding the women he'd told April were out there to teach him about love. He did, indeed, learn there was a lot more experience in the world of sexual thrills than he would ever find in her arms.

The women he found weren't devastated when he left. With a shrug of their shoulders, they said good-bye, confident someone else would be along to take his place. He couldn't recall a single one of them who cried when he left, not the way April had cried and begged him to stay.

A burst of applause startled him, and he blinked, aware that April was looking at him, a strained expression around her soft mouth.

As Russ turned away from her, she knew he was wondering about her obvious reluctance to remember who or what she was. Frowning, concentrating on what she had read on phenomena that enabled people to display symptoms by simply refusing to accept what was real, she stared unseeing at the clowns.

Maybe I have a doubtful past I'm trying to forget, she thought. *Maybe I killed someone. No, Elsa would tell me. Maybe it's something I kept hidden from Elsa. Perhaps a stolen husband.*

No. No stolen husband. She was so attracted to the man beside her that she was positive there was never another man who could interest her enough to steal from another woman. And Russ was divorced.

They were too young, he said. That was all he had said about his marriage. They were too young.

In a last blaring fanfare, the program ended, and she blinked as bright lights came on, turning to look at the man beside her.

"We might as well sit here a moment, April," Russ leaned over to tell her. He was still holding her hand.

She nodded, watching the sea of people move toward the exits. It was half an hour later before they reached his car.

As he inched from the parking area along with hundreds of other patient drivers, he asked, "Did you enjoy it?"

"Oh, yes. Thank Mr. Calloway for me. The seats were great."

"Yes, I'll be sure to tell him," he said, his voice going distant again.

I'm not the only strange one, she thought. *Russ has some strange ways about him. Maybe not. Maybe this is normal for him.* But the hurt she could almost feel herself? No one carried hurt like that in a normal sense.

"Would you like a drink?" he asked into the lengthy silence.

"No, thank you," she said, wondering if she ever drank. She was thirsty for some ice water, not anything alcoholic, she was sure. She stilled herself for his good-bye as he parked the car and came around to open her door. They walked side by side up the narrow steps to the door of her apartment.

"May I come in?" he asked. "It isn't too late for you?"

She shook her head, glancing at her watch as she turned the lights on inside. It was not yet midnight on a Saturday night, with no scheduled run until Monday.

"Hi, fella," she said, and bent to rub Brush as he bounced from the couch. Generous with his greetings, which included Russ, he settled down on the floor near the end of the couch, head on paws to watch them.

"I could make us some coffee, but mine's terrible," she told him, smiling at her own candid admission. "I want some water."

"I'm not thirsty. Go ahead and get you some ice water." He followed her across the small room and leaned against the counter as she took a glass from a shelf, put ice cubes in it and ran water from the faucet. They stood facing each other as she drank and placed the glass on the counter.

"April," he said softly.

She had half turned from him, and now her head swung around as he called her name. His hand on her arm brought her about to hold her in front of him. To keep her balance, she put her hands up to his chest, and as she stared up into his face, her fingers curled, gathering the material of his shirt to hold on.

His lips parted as though to say something else, but he lifted her up on tiptoes, her mouth just below his. He kept her there for a poignant second that lasted forever, his breath cool on her face. As he lowered his head to put his lips over hers, the painful tightness in her chest lessened, allowing her to breathe.

His mouth fit hers as she had known it would, leaving its imprint as though it had been made to rest easily on the softness of hers. His name didn't escape from her throat but was only a sound he caught with his kiss.

His hand slid down her back, pressing her hips into him, holding her closer than she thought possible. Her hands released his shirtfront to slide around his neck, and her fingers spread across the back of his thick hair. One hand slid away from his neck to curve over his ear, her little finger touching and entering the outer rim to rub into the smoothness there.

Her body detached itself from her thoughts, floating in liquid fire as his hands found parts to caress, his fingers dividing as they came around under her breasts, circling the swelling mounds beneath the soft material of her dress. His lips moved from her mouth, leaving a moist trail with the tip of his tongue to the soft spot near her temple, pushing away a strand of hair to find her ear. His tongue took him through the narrow tender passages to the earlobe, and she gasped as he nibbled it.

Her strength drained away as she lay powerless against him. She tried to say his name, but his mouth was back on hers, hard and not to be denied. Her lips answered his, paying no attention to the thought she must stop him. One hand curled into his hair, the other one along his cheek, her thumb rubbing back and forth. Her hips, using the same rhythm, moved from side to side, sensing his steamy desire for her, crushed to him so that neither could ignore the fact.

She didn't want to deny it; she wanted to lose herself in the lightning strokes of heat set off by their bodily contact, wanted to give in to the savage intensity they aroused in each other.

Suddenly, her lips were free, and Russ was holding her arms at her sides, staring down into her face. His eyes were hidden by lids that were almost closed, by the thick brown lashes lying straight against his cheek. The mouth that had freed hers in that instant was twisted, whether in desire for her or anger at himself, she couldn't tell.

He pulled her roughly to the couch and pushed her down to stand over her, his eyes taking in the dress front that had come unbuttoned as his hands explored, staring into the wide brown eyes filled with wild desire he awakened in her.

His hands clenched at his sides, long arms held loosely alongside his slim frame. It was a familiar stance she remembered, one she was used to seeing, one that invited the fitting of her own slender body into its angles.

Her heart was beginning to slow down, but her body trembled as she watched the fleeting expression cross his features. One hand reached upward toward him, and after a moment he took it, sitting on the couch beside her.

His mouth worked. "It was a mistake seeing you again, April. I knew it was the wrong thing to do, but I couldn't stay away from you, knowing there were things you were so uncertain about since the accident." He held her hand to his chest, working her fingers back and forth with his own. Just the touch sent warmth flowing through every nerve end.

"But Russ, I wanted to see you. Why...?" She stopped.

He was shaking his head. "I don't just want to see you, April. I want you. You understand? There's quite a difference." A smile touched his mouth. "It's been little more than a week since you lost your identity—a few days that have driven me crazy trying to stay away from you."

She was sure, as sure as she would ever be. This man sitting beside her was the reason she never dated, the reason Wade Outen never convinced her she should go out with him. She had been waiting for Russ all her life; without knowing who she was or remembering that he was at one time a family friend, she knew he was the one she would love to the exclusion of all others.

"Oh, Russ," she said, sitting up and leaning toward him, forcing him to take her other hand to hold both of hers with both of his. "It's all right. Even if it has been only a week, it's all right."

"Wait, April—"

"No," she whispered. "No. I don't want to wait. Hold me."

I have to tell her, he was thinking. *I have to let her know about us. Not now,* something warned. *Wait.*

With a groan, he released her hands to pull her to him, and slowly his hands moved over her body, feeling the trembling go through her. They went across her shoulders and down her back to fit over the curving hips, alongside her thighs. She leaned against the back of the couch, pulling him with her. Her slippers had fallen off, and she brought her leg up so that he fit into the entire length of her body, feeling the strength of his growing need for her.

His breath mingled with hers as he pushed her down into the couch cushions, and she took him with her. He moved until his face fit into her throat, lips caressing the hollow at the base, trailing to the small valley between her breasts.

Feelings aroused by his touch were remembered sensations, each move one she had sensed before; tiny kisses breathed life into millions of nerve ends over the surface of her body. She lay still, a smile curving her mouth as he explored the soft swell of her breast. His breath caught audibly as he found the hardened peak, and his hand curved beneath it, holding firmly as his tongue traced around the darker flesh.

Her breath was shallow, held quiet so as not to endanger the flaming rivers washing over her. Russ was exploring her body, and she wanted him to; she wanted him to know every inch of her slim firmness that she couldn't recall a man ever knowing.

"Honey?" He lifted his head, and she reached to place her hands on each side of his face, stroking the craggy features. With her forefinger, she rubbed across his wide mouth, feeling the beginning of a rough beard as her hand drifted over his chin.

"This feeling, Russ. The way you make me feel— I've been waiting for it." She didn't look into his eyes, instead following the path of her fingers as they explored his face—over the thick brows, the lines at the corner of his mouth, smoothing the hair back from his forehead.

A soft look of wonder came into her eyes as she widened them to gaze into his light blue ones. They weren't as light just then, but had darkened with his desire for her.

His breath was still uneven, his hand still curved around the breast he had discovered so receptive to his kisses. His thumb slowly moved across the tightly coiled tip he massaged so easily—a remembered caress that had always brought a warm response from April.

The smile slowly disappeared from her lips as he bent once more to touch them. His lips, slightly parted, fitted over her lower one, his tongue outlining the moist softness, triggering a silver streak of light from his touch. Her thighs quivered as she pressed them upward into the hardness of his body, and the silver streak became a lightning bolt as he forgot to be gentle, his kiss demanding that her entire being be given into his keeping.

She was aware of the dress being pushed from her shoulders, sliding over her hips, disappearing from the couch. Eagerly, she answered his urgently seeking mouth, his adventuring hands. His shirt opened beneath her questing fingers, pushed away to allow her hands to sweep over the roughness of the hair curled over the wide expanse of his chest.

Losing her breath to his seeking mouth, she gave in to the leaping flames, knowing they would consume her. Not just her; she would be consumed with Russ, and that was what had to be. He was hers, as she was his, exploring her, demanding her complete surrender, urging her toward the consummation of the flaming desire for each other.

Russ lifted her from the confines of the couch, and she held on as he stretched her on the carpeted floor.

"My belt," he said, not releasing her mouth.

Struggling a little with the hard leather to unfasten it, she finally pulled it free, sliding the zipper of his pants down as she did so. He groaned as she sought his naked flesh beneath his clothing.

"Sweetheart, do you—" He lifted his head to look down into her face. Her dark eyes were wide open; her lips were bruised and moist, still parted from his kisses. He hesitated, his eyes taking in the desire plain in her expression. "Will it be all right?"

"I don't know," she said, realizing what he was asking her. "I've never—" She reached for him. "I don't care. Don't leave me."

He lay beside her, turning her body to his, holding her close. Thin panties separated them; that was all. His breathing was harsh as his hands slid over her smooth shoulders, down to the small waist. One finger went beneath the elastic of her panties and stopped.

Hungrily, her mouth sought his again, and he allowed her tongue its demanding entrance inside. His hand went upward to tangle in the thickness of her hair, and for a moment they were locked in each other's arms.

Only for a moment. The hand caught in her hair gently pulled her head away from him. A big hand touched her cheek; she could feel the roughness of his fingertips at the corner of her mouth.

The sharp breath she drew in was ragged, coming from deep inside her chest, hurting as she felt his withdrawal.

"Me, too, April," he whispered, in answer to the intense desire he saw in her dark eyes. "I can't bear to leave you this way, wanting me as I want you. Take my word for it, honey. It's the hardest thing I've ever done." He smiled a little as he continued to look into her wide eyes.

He shook his head. "But tomorrow you might be sorry. I would never want you to be sorry for giving me your love." He caressed her lips with the rough-tipped finger. "We can't take a chance that you aren't protected. Oh, darling," he said, pulling her head beneath his chin, his lips pressed to her hair. They lay still as the glowing flames inside them grew quiet, waiting.

A long time later he moved. He sat up, pulling her with him, his gaze going over the firm swelling of her breasts. He bent his head and pressed his lips between them. Then he was standing, taking her with him, turning her away.

"Get a housecoat on before I change my mind," he told her, walking across the room to the sink. He ran water into the glass she had used and drank deeply.

April watched him for a moment, then started toward the closet where her robe hung. She had to step over Brush, who had watched the entire episode with his head on his paws.

Swallowing over the sudden fright in her throat, she stood at the closet door, unable to identify the robe through the mist in her eyes. She was frightened at the intensity of the feelings Russ aroused in her.

Russ was almost a total stranger, perhaps a friend of the family, but many years ago. A total stranger who took her to dinner and the circus, who made love to her until she neither knew nor cared if she had ever loved before, until she was willing to take a chance that she might get pregnant if their desire was consummated.

Russ, a stranger but still a stranger who knew the dangers they faced, wasn't willing. She was lucky.

Reaching blindly into the small dark space, her hands found the flannel material of her robe, and she withdrew it, wrapping it around her before she turned to face Russ across the room.

He was watching her, and as she turned, he placed the glass on the counter and walked toward her. They met by the couch, and both his hands came out to her.

"April," he said, and stopped. He held her hands tightly between both of his. The pain was in his eyes, the lines of controlled anguish bracketing the wide mouth. The mouth that was so tender on hers, the lips that lifted her into paradise, forbidden paradise, for she had no knowledge of whether she used birth control.

She didn't know anything about April Hayden, and Russ Calloway would take no chances. She was lucky.

Biting her lower lip, she looked up at him and saw him flinch as his eyes followed the movement.

"I'm sorry—" she started to say, but he shook his head.

"I'm the one who's sorry, April. I knew what would happen; I wanted it to happen." He smiled, bending to kiss the top of her head. "We'll have to be very careful from now on."

Releasing her hands, he reached for his shirt, buttoning it and pushing it beneath his loose belt, fastening it, his eyes still on her face. Turning away toward the door, he didn't see her hands reach automatically to hold him.

At the door he looked back at her. "Be careful on your trip. Good night, April." He was gone, the door clicking shut behind him, his footsteps echoing on the steps going downstairs. She stood still until she heard the car door slam and the motor start. It was quiet as the car pulled away into the distance.

Brush got up and came to stand in front of her, head lifted to inform her it was time for a walk. It was one o'clock Sunday morning. She followed the frisky dog downstairs and waited for him to return.

Together, they walked up the stairs, entered the one room they called home and minutes later went to bed on the couch that had held the man who was a stranger as he made love to her, the stranger she was beginning to love.

Chapter Eight

There was a single light burning in the front room of the Calloway house as Russ parked his car in the driveway. His mother, knowing he was safe and would be home again that night, felt secure to go to bed and leave a light on for him.

His key fit the lock of the front door as easily as it ever did, and he closed it quietly behind him, standing a moment in the uncarpeted hallway, listening for any sound that would say his parents were still awake.

Stepping lightly, he went into the living room. Except for the pictures, it looked much the same as it had for years. Only two pictures stood on the mantel now. One of him had been taken a few years back, when he returned from Hong Kong where he had been on a special project; another was a recent one from the Associated Press report on the kidnapping and release.

There was a time when the mantel held pictures of April and him: their high school graduation pictures—his four years ahead of hers, their engagement pictures and the wedding photograph. He wondered what his mother had done with them; they disappeared before he made his first return trip back to the United States after he went to work for ARCOT. What had April done with their picture albums? He still had the set of rings she returned when the divorce was final.

He hadn't thought about getting her wedding rings back and was surprised at the hurt he felt because she didn't want to keep them. The small package had been waiting for him his first trip back from overseas, and by that time he would have given anything to be able to convince April to wear them again. But he hadn't been able to find any trace of her.

His fingers fumbled as he unbuttoned the shirt April had opened. He slipped it off, dropping it on the back of a chair. It smelled of April's light cologne or her hair; he couldn't distinguish it.

Wandering around the room, he stopped by the fireplace that held remaining warmth from the ashes of the fire left by his parents. Taking the poker from the rack, he pushed a small piece of log onto the red coals and watched it blaze. He took a log from the side of the hearth and placed it on top, waiting for it to catch before he sat in the big chair his dad always used. Stretching his feet across the hassock, he stared into the flames licking around the log, his mind on April Hayden, who long ago had been April Calloway.

They had been young, young and so much in love they couldn't see anything or anyone but each other. Eighteen-year-old April, hero-worshiping twenty-two-year-old Russ. Since she was twelve, she was always underfoot, just there, unnoticed because she was a kid, a kid who turned sixteen, seventeen and a lovely eighteen he couldn't live without.

He was the one who grew dissatisfied. In college the guys were always talking about the "older" women they dated, the latest dates with the campus queen.

April's arms were warm and loving, but she was just a child, and he began to think she'd never grow up. He had a child bride he was still bringing up as though he were the parent.

Looking back, he saw himself as the immature, childish one and April the one who had grown up ahead of him. But at the time she hadn't been enough for him.

His conscience bothered him; he had never been free of April as he wanted to be. And for a while he hated her for it. He remembered the disbelief when he told her she was smothering him to death, the wild grief in her when, in spite of all she could do to convince him, he left her. He couldn't forget any of it.

He had accomplished everything he set out to do— and more. Master's degree in hand, he had accepted the position with ARCOT and never regretted it. They had been generous with salary, with raises, with benefits. With their liberal educational policies he had gone for his doctorate and gained another substantial increase in his income.

To achieve his total freedom, he got a divorce, leaving April free to do as she pleased without feeling tied to him.

He filed for divorce, and the nightmares started. To appease what he thought was an attack of conscience, he sent her money to continue her schooling. For two years he sent generous checks until she would have received her college degree. He stopped the checks, but he couldn't stop his thoughts from returning again and again to April.

He wrote to her only once, sending it to the apartment they'd shared as man and wife for three years. It came back marked Addressee unknown.

His job responsibilities increased; he was on the road seventy-five percent of the time—no schedule fit for a family—and so he never grew serious enough with any girl to think of marriage. It would be vastly unfair to tie anyone down to a husband gone from home so much of the time. A family needed roots.

Despite all his efforts to kill his love for April, even though he thrust it brutally away from him so he could seek a deeper, more satisfying, mature relationship with an older woman who knew the ropes, somehow it survived. He'd been the first man for April, and aside from brief experiments as a teenager that left him vaguely dissatisfied with sexual relations, she was the first woman for him.

There had to be more; April was a youngster, an amateur when it came to lovemaking. He needed a woman to bring his desires to fulfillment. He bit his lip, remembering.

How wrong he'd been. No one ever came close to the feelings April could rouse in him.

As the years passed, she retreated into his subconsciousness, always there when he let down his guard, coming to haunt his dreams when he grew unwary, always in his heart, protected by the years of loving her.

The kidnapping by the terrorists brought him about-face to the fact that life was too important a commodity to be left useless and empty of love. April stayed with him the desperate and frightening nights in the dungeon where only rats kept him company. She was there on the days they threatened him with death if the company didn't comply with their demands. He held on to her, the only sane thing in a world gone crazy.

He made up his mind then that if he got out of the predicament alive, he'd find April. Somewhere there must be someone who knew her, who would remember the slender girl he was once married to, her dark brown laughing eyes and lighter brown hair swinging to her shoulders. Even if she was married, he needed to know what she was doing and if life turned out well for her.

His release had been unexpectedly quick; the company came through, and the terrorists had at least kept their part of the bargain and let them go. It had been twelve days of hell for him and Winton, the engineer kidnapped with him. Winton's wife and children waited for him; he had only his parents. April wasn't waiting.

Funny, his parents never mentioned April, and when something came up that might involve her, they quickly changed the subject. He didn't pursue it, thinking they, like he, were saddened by the loss of the girl they had loved and didn't wish to make it harder on him. Nothing anyone did could make it harder than he made it on himself.

It had been impossible to avoid the local publicity when he arrived home and was asked to make appearances. He didn't accept them all, but he admitted to himself that he hoped April would see him and perhaps call to say she was glad he was home.

Instead, April made the papers in an accident. At least it had helped him find her even if she didn't know who she was.

He was surprised to see she still drove the old car his parents had helped them pay for. It was in good condition, but it seemed odd that after so many years she still owned it. Very few people kept a car nine years no matter how good a condition it was in.

"Maybe if you and Dad went to see April, it might trigger something to help, Mother," he'd said one night at dinner.

To his surprise, his mother's eyes filled with tears, and she got up and left the table. His dad stared after her and cleared his throat uncomfortably. "I guess Mother thinks we should have made more effort to see April over the years," he said. "But we thought it best—"

"I know, Dad. You're probably right." He went on eating, wondering about his mother, who had loved April as her own, or so he had thought.

The log on the fire burned through and broke, sending a shower of sparks up the chimney. He stirred in the chair, glancing at his watch. He had been woolgathering for two hours. Now his mind went back to something more recent, back to the hours after dinner and the circus, back to April in his arms, still in his blood, able to make that blood boil with desire for her.

April would have given herself to him tonight—the way April would always have done. For once he wasn't selfish with her; for once he thought of April instead of only himself.

How would she react when she regained her memory and found that he was her former husband, the husband who had deserted her, thrown her love and affection back in her face in his juvenile search for a mature love unknown to young April?

Even with amnesia, how could April not feel the deep love he had for her? Why couldn't the emotional tug-of-war going on inside of him awaken her to the fact she had once loved him?

Once? What if that were the only chance he ever had with April?

Often he had heard people wish for another chance to do something in the past a different way. Regret. Plain wishful thinking. He now knew what they meant. If he could know then what he knew now, April would still be his. If he had grown up when he was supposed to, he would never have hurt her.

Somewhere in the house the hour of two o'clock chimed softly. His entire body ached with wanting April.

I should have taken her while I could, he thought, *and asked her forgiveness later.* When she finally remembered who she was, would he be able to convince her of his love?

He buried his face in his hands and groaned.

Chapter Nine

Her body felt unnaturally light. It was as though Russ held and caressed her even as she lay alone on the couch. Her cheeks burned as she recalled her response to him, her eagerness to belong to him, as though it were the right thing to do, as though she knew it was right for her to belong to Russ.

She twisted. *He must think I do that all the time,* she thought, burying her hot face in the pillow. *Maybe I do.* She moaned softly and sat up, drawing the light blanket up to her chest. Beside her, Brush stirred and moved closer to her.

She patted his head. "I'm not going to leave you, Brush. You're the only thing I know for sure belongs to me."

Who is April Hayden? Where does she fit into the scheme of things? Russ Calloway's life was settled, his plans out in front, with an important career assured.

He didn't talk much about the kidnapping, and she didn't know enough about it or his company to ask questions. It was most likely a bad experience he didn't want to discuss just yet. She could understand that.

What she didn't understand was the feelings he roused in her. It was almost as though she knew his arms, knew the response that ricocheted through her body. His wide mouth belonged on hers, his hands fit so many places on her body she was sure no one else knew existed.

She wanted him; oh, how she wanted him to stay with her. But Russ thought only of protecting her. She smiled and slid beneath the covers again. There was more than just wanting his own satisfaction if he thought of her first.

As late as it was when she went to sleep, she was awake early. Stopping only to pick up a Sunday morning paper, she drove to the truck stop.

"Place's full, Brush," she told the small dog. "Wonder if Sundays are always like this?"

Inside, she glanced around, and when someone waved, she waved back as she made her way to the counter where Elsa was talking to some of her customers.

"Hi, April. How's the head?"

"Still fuzzy," she told her, grinning back, meeting the dark eyes of the man sitting on the next stool.

Elsa looked from April to the man. "This is Wade Outen, April."

Turning to face him, she looked him over as she nodded. There wasn't even the vaguest glimmer of recognition. "Hello, Wade," she said.

"Well, April, since you don't know me, I can start off fresh without your standard 'No, thanks' answer to my usual 'How about dinner tonight?'" He watched to see if that made any impression. It didn't.

She laughed, anyway. "I always say no?"

"That's right. Maybe a yes would change your luck and you could remember why you always said no."

His appearance was neat; he was clean; he wasn't bad looking. "You have no idea why I say no?" she teased.

He shook his head. "I think you may be stubborn, but I'm not sure." He grinned, showing straight white teeth.

Elsa placed a cup of coffee in front of her, and she sipped it thoughtfully. *Because of Russ Calloway,* she thought, and stiffened. She hadn't known Russ Calloway long enough for him to interfere with her going out with anyone else. She had known him a week— didn't even know him. Acquainted was the word she needed in connection with Russ.

Last night, in his arms, it was as though she had known him a long time. Even now her body responded to the feel of his hands finding their way over her, stripping away the shadows hiding her identity.

Last night she knew who she was: a woman lost in the feelings roused by a man she had known a week— uninhibited emotions seeking fulfillment from a stranger.

The door behind her opened, and she lifted her head quickly to look into the mirror over the counter. It wasn't Russ, and she pushed aside the disappointment that flared.

"April?" Beside her, Wade was talking.

"Yes, Wade?"

"Yes?"

"Well…" She laughed. "I'm sorry. What did you say?"

He slid off the stool and put a bill on the counter. "What I said was I'll see you next weekend. I'm on my way to Shreveport."

"Have a good trip, Wade," she said automatically. He grinned and left.

Russ didn't come in, and she ate her breakfast wondering about him. A dinner, a circus and two hours of lovemaking that ended before she wanted it to end were the sum total of her knowledge of Russ Calloway. She paid for her meal and left.

Early spring in California was beautiful, she decided as she let Brush out of the car for a moment before turning the old vehicle toward her apartment. It was a cloudless day, with the sun coming up over the eastern ridge of the city.

Once inside the apartment, she stood looking around—a very small area for a woman, even a woman alone. April Hayden certainly didn't require much space. She frowned.

Russ Calloway filled up all the empty niches in her mind as well as the room. What kind of home did he have? When she saw him again— Maybe he wouldn't come back.

She spread the paper out beside her and concentrated on the day's news. There was a slight empty place inside her, and she grew vaguely angry that she missed seeing Russ Calloway enough to make a big difference in her day.

Instead of going to the truck stop for dinner, she left Brush in the apartment and drove to the northern outskirts of the city to a restaurant she had noticed on her trip on Friday. She was back home by the time it grew dark. The phone didn't ring, although she sat and stared at it, willing it to do so.

Her scheduled trip to San Diego would keep her away from home two nights and most of three days. The temptation to call Russ before she left was great, but she fought it without knowing why. He didn't seem the type who would enjoy having a woman chase him if he didn't show a lot of interest in her.

She couldn't begin to figure him out. There wasn't enough experience—or memory of experience—behind her to help in analyzing him. All she could do was remember the feelings he left with her on Sunday morning.

MONDAY, the beginning of a workweek and routine she fit in as though she knew who she was. Habit, she decided, enabled her to do whatever had to be done. It was early when she set her speed on the interstate going south toward San Diego.

She signed for a room at the truckers' quarters after dropping off her trailer load and strolled along the street, looking into windows. At the corner store she stopped, going inside to look for a paperback novel to keep her company. She found an interesting-looking cover and looked around for the cashier.

Down the aisle she found a counter that said ''feminine hygiene'' and stopped. A plastic holder near eye level held a pamphlet with a heading that mentioned family planning.

Biting into her lower lip, she finally reached up to take one of the leaflets, scanning instructions written there. According to the author, there were few really safe contraceptives. Safe meaning effective. Consult your own physician.

And if one has no physician, April wondered. What then?

Suddenly conscious of what she was doing, she replaced the leaflet, turned and walked quickly to the cash register to pay for her book.

Outside, she hurried back toward the truck stop and was breathing rapidly when she got to the small room reserved overnight for her. She sat on the bunk, rubbing the back of her neck. Russ Calloway was becoming an obsession with her.

The book proved to be interesting enough to keep her mind half on it, anyway, and before midnight she turned out her light and went to sleep.

The next morning she signed on for a return load, glad it would give her something to think about on the ride back. You have to pay attention when you're pulling a load; when empty, there's a tendency to let your mind wander, and she had no desire to have her mind taking over with things she shouldn't be thinking about.

It was late when she checked in at Maxwell's, and she went as far as the posted schedules to see when she left on the next trip. Tomorrow, an overnight trip to San Bernardino.

There were no messages for her; Russ had not called. Glancing into the café, she saw Katie moving around but not Elsa. She went home.

Even though she willed the phone to ring, it didn't. She stayed away from the telephone book to keep from checking to see if the Calloways' number was listed. If he wanted to talk to her, he'd call.

Sighing, she decided she had read much more into his kisses than Russ meant for her to. She twisted and turned herself into a restless sleep, glad when the radio clock beside the couch came on and she could drag herself up to go to work.

"Back tonight, April?" Elsa asked her as she put the usual breakfast plate in front of her.

"Tomorrow, but I should be in early. I'm taking a load of camping equipment to San Bernardino."

"Russ came in for breakfast yesterday morning. Guess he forgot you'd still be gone."

"Probably," she agreed aloud. *No, he didn't forget,* she told herself.

It was still dark as she drove south, the kind of day she loved. With Brush beside her, she was always content on the road. Must be spring fever that made her so restless. She pushed away the feeling, concentrating on her driving.

A tiny pain edged its way along the scar in her eyebrow, and she reached up to touch it in surprise. It hadn't hurt since the stitches were taken out. After a moment, the ache eased off, and she forgot about it as the miles piled up on top of each other.

Delivery and return trip were made without incident, and she was back at the truck stop, parking her rig, by seven o'clock Friday evening. A load of boating equipment for Lake Tahoe was her only agendum for Saturday—not even a full day's work. Monday's schedule would take her back to Susanville, across the mountain where the accident occurred.

Inside the café, she glanced around, then found an empty booth near the back window. She was tired, and the uncomfortable feeling around the scar was more irritating than painful. It just let her know it was there.

Elsa waved to her, and Katie took her order. As soon as she was given a glass of water, she swallowed two aspirins, leaned back in the booth and closed her eyes.

"April?"

The voice of so many dreams. Her eyes flew wide as she stared up at Russ. She straightened in the seat, taking in the neat figure in jeans and long-sleeved blue shirt.

"Hello, Russ."

"May I?" he asked, indicating the seat opposite her.

She nodded. *How formal,* she thought. *Perhaps we're starting over.*

"Are you in for the weekend?" he asked, his eyes traveling from her open-collared denim shirt to the rolled-up cuffs.

"I have a run tomorrow," she told him.

"Do you work every weekend?"

"Not always. It's only to Lake Tahoe. I'll be through by midafternoon."

He continued to look at her, his eyes missing none of her facial features, and she found herself coloring beneath his steady gaze. Becoming conscious of staring, he looked away toward Katie, moving among the tables, and back to her.

"Have you ordered?"

"Yes. If you're hungry, the corned beef and cabbage is excellent." She smiled to let him know she realized they were making conversation for some reason she wasn't sure of.

As Katie came by, he took her suggestion, then leaned back to study her once more.

"Do you have any plans for tonight?"

She shook her head. "No." *Of course not,* she thought. *According to Elsa, I never have plans.*

"Are you too tired to see a movie?"

"No." She looked down at her denim shirt and jeans. "But I should change clothes."

He smiled for the first time. "It isn't necessary, I've noticed. Jeans are definitely what the best-dressed individual wears almost anywhere these days."

Katie came with big platters of corned beef and cabbage, and she realized she was actually hungry. She hadn't noticed until Russ joined her. Perhaps the change in atmosphere whetted her appetite.

They held hands in the movie; they ate popcorn; she grew teary and sentimental in places, and Russ squeezed her hand as she sniffed and used a tissue to blow her nose.

Outside, the wind had increased, and clouds obscured the stars. It smelled like rain. Her thick hair stirred with the increased breeze, and she wished she'd worn her jacket.

"Here comes the rain," he told her. "Run." Holding her hand, pulling her along the street toward the car, he laughed back at her as big drops hit them, followed by a downpour. They were wet by the time they got into his car.

"Whew! That was quick," she said, wiping her face with her hands and her hands on her jeans.

He didn't answer and she turned to look at him. In the semidarkness of the car his gaze was intent upon her, and as she lifted her face to him, he reached out.

Whatever he said was lost as his mouth found hers, the wetness of their cheeks cold as they touched. His hands found her, her outline in the tight jeans, the curves of her body beneath the shirt. He explored without restraint, knowing she wouldn't stop him. Her own hands searched for him, fingers digging into his chest.

She lost her breath as the tip of his tongue thrust inside the moist opening of her parted lips and cried out softly as he gathered her so close to him it hurt. Nothing warned her to stop; nothing cautioned against giving in to the trembling urgency in them both. The winds blew, and the rain poured down; the fires burned, and lightning flashed; the world spun madly, and he held her through it all.

His harsh breathing into her ear, his gentle push to get her head away from him, brought her back to earth. She couldn't see his face distinctly in the shadowy car, couldn't see any expression, but his heart beneath her ear pounded the same way hers did.

"Honey?"

She didn't answer, but her arms around him tightened; she did not want to give up the moment, refusing to lose him after a week without him.

"I'd better take you home," he whispered. "You're wet."

Both of them were wet. As he released her, she became aware of their wet clothing and shivered. He started the car and drove through the dark rain to her apartment.

Without a word, he took her hand, and they ran inside. Her teeth chattered as she waited for him to unlock the door, standing aside to allow her to enter. She had left the light on for Brush, and he came forward eagerly to welcome them home.

"Get those clothes off," Russ told her.

She pushed her wet hair back from her face. "How about you? You're as wet as I am."

"I just need a towel to dry my hair and face and I'll be okay."

Crossing the room to the bathroom, she reached inside the small shelf space to get a towel for him, turning back to find him right behind her.

He tilted her face upward and bent to kiss her on the mouth. he took the towel and dried her face, rubbed her hair, then looped the towel around his shoulders.

He concentrated on each button as he unfastened her shirt, the wet material hard to handle. As he pushed it from her shoulders, he wrapped the towel around them, letting his hands drop to unfasten her bra.

"Get those jeans off," he told her. "Is there a blanket in that closet?"

She nodded, and he moved around her to pull it from the shelf, throwing it across the couch as he faced her once more. The wet denim stuck to her, and she was forced to hold on to him as she pushed them down over her hips. He steadied her as she stepped out of them, taking the jeans from her hands as she straightened.

He went into the tiny bathroom, and she saw him put her jeans across the shower rod where they would drip without wetting the floor. He moved around the small area, performing tasks he seemed accustomed to doing.

When he came back toward her, he was smiling a little. He pushed her toward the couch, taking the blanket he had thrown there to put across her lap as she sat down.

"Y-you'd better get out of your clothes," she said.

"No, I'm going home," he said.

She wanted to protest, to ask him to stay, but she couldn't get the words out. He stood looking down at her, and in his eyes she saw the unhappiness that had been so evident the first time she saw him with Dr. Wall. The expression softened his features and deepened the lines around his mouth.

"You're going to Lake Tahoe tomorrow?" he asked.

She nodded.

"Can I see you tomorrow night?"

"Yes." She drew her lower lip between her teeth and saw him stiffen, jamming his hands into his wet pants pockets.

Turning quickly, he went toward the door. Brush followed him expectantly. With a questioning glance at her, then back at the dog, he smiled.

"I'd better take him downstairs first," he said, opening the door for Brush to walk out ahead of him.

They were back in a few minutes. She hadn't moved but sat huddled on the couch with the blanket completely around her.

"The rain's stopped. Maybe it'll be clear for your trip." He watched her a moment, then said, "Good night, April. I'll see you at seven."

She nodded. "Good night, Russ." She listened to his footsteps as he ran down the stairs away from her.

Brush sat up in front of her, button eyes pleading. She looked back at him a long moment before she realized he was telling her he was hungry.

"Sorry, Brush. I've been thinking of myself, not you." She dropped the blanket on the couch and took the towel from around her, replacing it with her robe. She looked at her nude body and shrugged.

Almost too slender, that body was achingly aware of missing Russ, of wanting the safe shelter of his long arms around it. Shivering, she remembered the hungry demands of his mouth and hands as he kissed her. The sadness in his eyes—what was he thinking of to look at her that way?

After feeding Brush, she leaned against the counter, looking around the room. It was familiar in a way, but in another way it was as though she stood in someone else's apartment. It was neat; the furniture, while not new, was of good quality.

It lacked personality and warmth, she decided. It was just a room, not really a home. She lived there, a stranger even to herself, knowing nothing about who she was or where she came from.

Russ knew her family, but they had been dead for years, and he had lived overseas a long time, divorced from the girl he was too young to marry. What was she like, this girl? What had happened to her after the divorce? He didn't say if she lived here or if she, too, had gone away after the divorce.

Russ hadn't really told her much more about himself than she was able to tell him about her. Strangers who pass, she thought. Strangers who pass in the night. Russ will pass through on his way to Australia, and she wouldn't know any more about him than she did when he was in Egypt working for ARCOT, where terrorists had held him for ransom before she even knew he existed.

The tiny nagging pain was back in the scar over her left eye. She took two aspirins, her thoughts still struggling with the enigma of one April Hayden who refused to come forward and be recognized.

Chapter Ten

Sitting across from Russ in the dimly lit restaurant, April was aware of the undercurrent beneath their conversation. He asked if she had any bad effects from getting wet; she said no. He asked about her trip to Lake Tahoe; she told him it was a beautiful drive. No, she wasn't tired.

Taking a sip from her water glass, she looked up to find his gaze going over her, taking in the different way she had fixed her hair, with a part on the side and swirled back in a heavy wave from her cheeks. The small amount of color she added to her cheeks and lips highlighted the darkness of her eyes.

On her way home from Maxwell's she had stopped by a dress shop, nervously trying to select something simple but attractive. She hadn't remembered what size she wore, but the salesgirl looked her over and picked one from the section marked "juniors." The label said size nine.

The dress was a deep lavender, almost straight but nipped in under her breasts, flaring outward over her hip bones, dropping just below her knees. A dainty white bow tied beneath the rolled collar, and a lacy cardigan sweater of lavender and white covered her bare arms. She pulled her lower lip between her teeth, giving him a tentative smile as he continued to look at her.

His eyes followed the familiar movement of her mouth, and his lips twisted slightly. ''Do you always leave Brush at home when you go out?''

She hesitated. ''I don't think I ever did before. He's good about being left but doesn't particularly like it.''

He nodded. ''I forgot again.''

''What?''

''That you don't always know what went on last month, last year, ever.'' He leaned forward, one hand reaching across to pick hers up where it lay on the table. ''Tell me how you can drive to all these places, find the delivery points, operate that rig—yet, you can't tell me what April Hayden was like before I met her.''

Her free hand went to her eye, and she drew her fingers along the almost-invisible scar at the edge of her eyebrow. It wasn't sore anymore, but the pain came almost often enough to be called frequent, and she had taken more aspirins than she wanted to in order to relieve it.

''Sometimes I almost remember,'' she said slowly, and realized that it was true. A shadowy recognition of something someone said, a motion she followed, a voice spoken without seeing the speaker. Even Russ— she raised her eyes to the uneven hairline, seeing the gray in the light brown waves of his hair.

Frowning, she tried to recall what it was about Russ that niggled at her memory. Maybe nothing; maybe it wasn't Russ but someone else. It could be Wade or any of the drivers she knew but somehow didn't know.

She turned her hand over and rubbed the palm over the roughness of his. "I should call Dr. Wall next week, I guess, and tell him the doctor here didn't find anything else wrong. That's something to be thankful for."

A young man brought their dinners, and Russ squeezed her hand lightly before withdrawing his. Across the table, their eyes met, and neither looked away for a long moment.

The waiter left them with a murmured "Enjoy your meal," and she drew in her breath, looking down at her plate. She wasn't sure if she was hungry anymore.

"Yes, we can be thankful for that," Russ said, and she looked up, not understanding, then realized he was commenting on her last statement. She nodded and picked up her fork.

Somehow she got through the meal, paying little attention to what she ate. Her every sense was aware of Russ across the table, and she was almost sure he was having the same trouble. Her thoughts went back to the night before when he had undressed her, taking her wet clothing away to give her a towel to dry, then a blanket to wrap around her nakedness.

Why did it seem so easy for him to do something like that? As though he knew what to do, how to hold her so she could take off the pants. Drying her, pushing her away, refusing to take advantage of the situation when she wished he had. It would have been so easy to step into his arms, to let him hold her. She was sure he had wanted to as much as she did.

"Ready?" he asked.

They had finished eating, and she had no idea what they had said or if they had said anything during the meal.

"Yes," she said, wiping her mouth with the napkin. She turned to pick up her bag, which was lying on the seat with her, and found that her hands were shaking. Following close behind him, she stood near the door, waiting until he paid the check, meeting his glance as he turned toward her.

For a moment they stood close together, looking at each other before he reached to push the door open for her to walk out ahead of him. In silence, he unlocked the door of the car, his hand lightly touching her elbow as she slid into the seat. She reached across to unlock his door and was leaning toward him as he settled behind the wheel.

In the dimness she saw him smile as he bent to place his mouth over hers. Long fingers cupped her chin to hold her there, sliding down her throat until his thumb touched the pulse throbbing there. He rubbed across the soft skin and took his hand away, raising his head to look down into her upturned face.

Without a word, he started the car, leaving her to draw in her breath to steady herself. She didn't know what to do with her hands and slid them beneath the handbag in her lap, curling her fingers together. It wasn't an awkward silence but one full of unspoken questions, full of thoughts from two people trying to sort out what should be said or left unsaid.

"April?"

Turning her head to look at him, she realized he had said something she didn't hear. "I—I'm sorry, Russ," she said, shaking her head. "I didn't understand you."

"I asked if we could go to a motel." His mouth twisted as she stared at him. "I know that sounds like a line from a cheap movie, but—"

The car was stopped, and she looked around at the unfamiliar street they were on. It was almost as though she were inside that movie he mentioned, watching someone act out their lines. She was frightened.

How ridiculous, she thought. *I'm twenty-seven, not sixteen. I've been with a man before....* She stopped, wondering how she knew that. Who was the man she was with before tonight?

She wet her lips, trying to find the right answer for him. "I don't want to go to a motel. Can we go to my place?"

"I wasn't sure you'd want to go there," he said, and when she didn't say anything, he started the car again and pulled away from where he had parked.

Walking in a vacuumlike mist, she preceded him up the stairs to her apartment, silently handing him her key. As he pushed the door open, Brush bounced forward, happy to see her returning to him.

Like an ordinary married couple, they moved around the big room. From the sink, she said over her shoulder, "If you'll open the couch, I'll feed Brush."

As she put the food in his dish, Brush went immediately to it, and she turned to look at Russ. He had opened the couch, and she looked at it, realizing she needed to get linens for it. Pulling them from the shelf, she stood opposite him to spread the sheets and put cases on the pillows.

She looked down at the small sleeping area. "It's too small for the two of us," she said.

He came around to her, reaching to pull her into his arms. "We're going to be close enough it won't matter." He tilted her face, and she was surprised at the pain registered in his eyes.

"Are you sure—?" she started to ask.

"Sure, April? Sure that I want you more than anything I've ever wanted in my life? Sure?" His arms tightened until she was so close to him, she couldn't move. "Oh, honey."

After a long moment of slowly crushing the breath from her, he pushed her away to look down at her. "And you, April? How do you feel? You look so scared." He pushed her hair back over her ear, letting the tips of his fingers caress gently along the rim. "Don't be afraid of me, honey. Don't."

The pleading in his eyes reminded her of something she had read or seen. She reached up to smooth the lines from around his mouth, and her fingers quietly traced his lower lip. As she withdrew her hand, he bent his head to kiss her. She breathed in his smell, a masculine fragrance she loved, not knowing if it was shaving lotion or male scent that was Russ.

At first, his mouth on hers was gentle, questioning, the edge of his teeth grazing her lips until they parted beneath his. At first, he led her, easing her down on the bed, one hand cupped behind her head to hold their lips together while the other one slid the zipper on the back of her dress and slipped the sweater away.

"Russ, I still don't know—" she whispered against his mouth. "I can't tell—"

"It's all right. I'll take care of you." His eyes were closed tightly, tangling thick lashes into a dark shadow beneath his eyes. His breath was rough coming from deep within his chest, stirring her hair as his lips moved along her cheek.

He pushed her down until she lay on the pillows, his hands behind her, unfastening her bra, slipping it from her arms. She stared up into his eyes, wide open now as he went over the smooth skin exposed to him. Her small breasts were almost flat as she lay on her back, waiting as he bent toward her.

He kissed each brown tip before he urged her hips upward to allow him to remove her dress and half slip. She wet her lips as she waited for him to hook his fingers beneath the panty hose, carefully removing them. He sat still, his gaze going over her body, finally leaning to place his lips in the center of her belly.

Her hands moved quickly to hold him there. "Russ."

He sat up, catching her hands to him. "Help me, darling."

As she fumbled with the small shirt buttons, he unfastened his belt. She watched, fascinated by his movements, as he stood up to remove his shoes and pants. He completed undressing and looked down at her.

"Move over a little, darling," he said, sitting on the edge of the bed.

He lay down, turning on his side to face her. Their hands went out at the same time to slide over each other. His big hand fit over the curve of her hip, pulling her all the way to him. The rigid evidence of his desire for her pushed into her flat belly.

"I want to love you, April. I want to hold you like this for hours, but I can't. I have to have you now; it's been so long—so long."

"Yes, oh, yes, Russ. I can't remember, but—"

His mouth cut her short. The mouth she had seen twisted in pain covered hers with gentle insistence, forcing her lips apart, finding her tongue to draw it to him. There hadn't been kisses like this, she was sure.

Hungry for him, she arched her body into the outline of his, hands moving quickly, learning the arrangement of his features, the muscles that moved beneath her questioning fingers.

With quiet insistence, he pushed her away from him, and when a small sound escaped her lips, he smiled down at her. "I need to see you, April," he said, stilling her protest. "I want to see what is mine."

"Yes," she said, giving in to his wishes. He bent to place his mouth over the brown tip that had swollen tightly, gasping as he drew his tongue across it. His hand moved down over her hip, curving across her thigh, stopping in the warmth of her legs she separated to allow him freedom to touch.

He raised himself up to look her over from head to toes and back to where his hand rested. Easing her legs apart, he bent to kiss her. With a slight thrust, his fingers went inside her, and her fingers on his shoulders dug into the hard muscles flexing beneath her hands.

There was no more waiting. He pulled away from her for a moment, but her eyes refused to open against the rapturous brilliance of shared desire. Where his fingers had been, another pressure began, another striving for entrance into her body.

Her eyes flew wide open to stare into his. "Honey?" His sudden thrust upward caught her by surprise, and she gasped, but his kiss came hard against her mouth as his body began a slow rhythmic push into her. Both his hands curved around her buttocks, holding her to receive his body as he forced himself deep inside her.

Her body began to undulate in a slow, sensuous response to Russ's demands. The tightness gave way to a fluid ease as they moved together. She felt the increased tenseness in his body as the building passion spilled over, and her body twisted as they cried out together. Shattering drumbeats thundered through her body, and lightning melted every fiber of her being before they lay still. He made no move to withdraw from her, and she was glad; she wanted to remain locked to him forever.

Hardly aware of any change in her senses, submerged in their soul-shattering release of passion, she finally roused enough to know that he was again moving inside of her.

Questioningly, she opened her eyes, still clinging to his arms. He smiled, placing his mouth over hers. Slowly, he sent his still-hard muscle in controlled thrusts within her well-lubricated body.

Her lashes settled over her eyes, no longer questioning. It was what she wanted, too, and he knew it. He lay still now, kissing her, biting into her lips, tracing her mouth with his tongue, sending the tip of it delightfully deep into her throat when she responded. Her arms tightened, and her body went from side to side beneath his.

His breathing became harder, and he was no longer lying still but withdrawing and reentering her with deep strokes. Wrapping her legs around him, she refused to let him leave her. With a groan, he gave in, and she felt the force of the expulsion he could no longer withhold. He rocked her gently back and forth and once again held her close as they clung together.

A long time later, he moved away, leaving her as he went into the bathroom. When he came back, he lay beside her, putting one arm across her body, lying curved where he had left her.

"Darling," he whispered. "April."

She didn't answer him, but in the darkness she smiled, moving her head down to his chest, feeling the roughness of the hair against her cheek. She put her hand up to his mouth, felt the quick breath against it and let it fall to his shoulder, placing her finger on the rushing pulse in his throat.

In the quiet darkness she lay held against the hard body that had claimed her for its own. It seemed so right—just the way it should be to belong to Russ. A man she had known only a week. But it seemed she had always known him, had always known the touch of his hands on her naked body.

Perhaps I belonged to him in another world, she thought. *Perhaps. . .* She smiled sleepily. Not in another world. She belonged to Russ in this world. It didn't matter that she had only met him a week ago. She belonged to him as much as if she had known him since childhood.

"Russ?" Her fingers traced a path up his arm, across his chest.

His voice was drowsy. "What, honey?"

She didn't pursue the conversation, satisfied that he was awake enough to think about the feelings they had shared. Feelings? It was an explosive happening, an earthshaking consummation of twin desires. Her body trembled, remembering.

"April?" His hand beneath her chin tilted it upward. "Is it all right?"

"Yes. Oh, yes, it's all right." She wriggled closer to him and felt his instant response against her belly. Her hand that had been resting on his hip slid downward to his hard thighs, dropping across the tautness he couldn't hide.

He breathed deeply, and she knew he was no longer drowsy. Surprised at the rush of heated response in her own thighs, she spread her fingers, holding him.

"Darling, unless you mean business—" he whispered finally as she played around over his hips, his thighs, his belly.

"Isn't this pleasure, Russ?" she asked, laughing softly. "I thought—" Her breath was crushed from her as his open mouth caught over hers, flicking his tongue inside the moistness. Opening and closing his mouth over hers until stars flashed beneath her closed lids, until she squirmed uncontrollably in his embrace.

"Surrender, sweetheart?"

"Yes, yes, yes," she crooned.

He filled her with a sweetness unknown to her before Russ. He took her into himself as he went into her. And when the flames could no longer be held back, they were consumed together in the raging fires built just for them.

RUSS STOOD outside April's apartment, looking back at the building, turning to see her little dog racing back toward him.

She's still mine, he thought, the exultant feeling making him feel more alive than he could remember in years.

Close on that thought came the memory that April didn't know she'd ever belonged to him. To her, it was the first time. It was almost like the first time for him, the first time ever of holding her body, alive and loving him without restraint.

He passed his hand over his eyes, the dark thoughts of his days with the kidnappers intruding where he didn't want them. But that was where he had used April to keep him sane when all else failed. Now he was using her again. What an odd word; a word that suited what he was doing, because April didn't know she'd once belonged to him. She was his, willing to love him as she'd always done.

Tell her, something inside him urged. *Tell her now; it will help her get over her uncertainty. No,* came the denial. *Not just yet.*

Snapping his fingers at Brush, he opened the car door to let him get in with him and headed for a coffee shop.

DREAMING, reaching for Russ, she opened her eyes quickly when her hands found empty space beside her on the bed. She sat up, glancing around at the empty room. Even Brush was gone. She looked back at the pillow next to hers. The imprint of Russ's head was there; it hadn't been a dream. He had loved her to the exclusion of all else. Their belonging to each other was real. A fierce streak of latent desire literally shook her slender body.

The sheet was gathered around her, only partially shielding her nakedness. Wonderingly, she looked around.

A light knock touched her door. "April?" Even as Russ called her, he was fitting the key into the lock. The door was pushed open, Brush bounded in, and Russ closed the door quickly. His eyes went over her as she sat staring, wide-eyed at him.

He was carrying a bag from a fast-food place. "I thought you might want some coffee," he said, smiling as he placed the bag on the counter.

She nodded. Brush stood nearby for her to rub him, then went to get a drink of water.

"Thank you for taking Brush out." She wet her lips and drew the lower one between her teeth. "He probably feels neglected."

"He enjoyed the ride, I think," he said, coming toward her with a steaming cup of coffee for her.

"Did you get cream?" she asked.

"I put cream in yours," he said, and for a moment an odd look came into his eyes. "I saw you use it at the restaurant."

"Oh, yes, but I wasn't sure you'd remember," she said, sipping the hot liquid. "It's good. I make terrible coffee."

He laughed. "Is that right? I thought anyone could make coffee."

"Maybe so, but not necessarily fit to drink." She settled back against the pillow, holding the sheet so that her breasts were covered, leaving her shoulders bare.

He sat on the side of the bed, watching her. His eyes took in the shape of her beneath the sheet, coming back to rest on her mouth. He moved closer and bent to kiss her.

"It's been a long time," he said.

She drew in a sharp breath. "A long time since what?"

He closed his eyes tightly for an instant; then he was smiling at her. "A long time since I last kissed you." She looked hard at him, and gradually the smile faded from his face. "Hurry and drink your coffee so I don't have any longer to wait."

Tentatively, she took another drink, then placed it on the floor by the bed. "Now?" she asked.

"Now," he said, and reached for her.

The sheet slid from around her, exposing the ginger brown tips to his tender gaze. Each of his hands cupped a firm mound, his thumbs circling the dark crest. His mouth on hers was a sensual movement from corner to corner, his tongue lightly probing into her mouth as he stopped to reverse his quest.

With little urging from him, she lay back on the pillows, pulling him with her. His clothing hastily discarded, he lowered himself beside her, holding her close as he whispered words that sent her senses soaring to collide with his, shook her body as he once more entered her, set them adrift in the flames once more, eagerly absorbing each other, drenching the flames with their love.

Her body still trembled long after they lay wrapped in each other's arms. The steady rise and fall of his chest beneath her ear lulled her into half sleep.

It was a long time later when he got up and heated their coffee.

Chapter Eleven

He didn't leave her all day Sunday. After they drank the reheated coffee, they dressed and went out for breakfast, buying a paper as they left the restaurant. Back in the tumbled bedclothes on the couch, they divided the paper.

"Here's an advertisement from ARCOT," she said. "They want a chemical engineer for a position in Egypt."

"That's the one I had," he said quietly.

She lowered the paper. "Would you mind going back over there?"

"I'd rather not go back just yet. Perhaps after I finish the job in Sydney, I might think about it."

He was reading the cartoons as she watched him, absorbed in the lines around his mouth that she had smoothed away for a time last night, and this morning.

She smiled as he looked up at her. "Australia's about to have its wintertime now, isn't it?"

"Yes. They have opposite seasons from us."

Turning her attention back to the paper, she lost interest in the want ads. Soon Russ would be leaving going halfway around the world to a new job in Australia, far away from the frightening experience at the hands of terrorists, far away from April.

Laying the paper aside, she stretched out beside him, turned so that she could watch his facial expressions as he read the comics. He was so serious.

He became aware of her gaze and smiled at her, reaching over to brush her hair back as he leaned to kiss her on the nose. He started to look back at his paper, but his gaze encountered hers, and they stared at each other.

The paper slid from his hands, and he rolled over to fit himself against her. He shifted her so that one of his arms was beneath her head, the other one thrown across her. His kiss brushed her lips in a fleeting caress that roused her body like a live wire. Pulling away enough to look into her face, he smiled, nestling her head beneath his chin, and they went to sleep.

She was still holding him when he moved, a spasmodic jerk, slinging his hand outward and moaning as he pressed closer to her. Then he was fighting, throwing his hands up, pushing her to the floor out of his arms. He cried out, waking himself, staring in tortured anger at her as she sat by the couch, watching him.

"April," he whispered. "What happened?"

She climbed back into the bed beside him, putting her arms around him, talking softly. "You were dreaming?" she asked after a while.

His arms tightened. "Yes. They were going to beat us again."

His breathing quieted, and she closed her mind to what he must have gone through, hiding the terror in her at the thought of Russ being tortured by the kidnappers. A long time later, he slept, still holding her.

LATE AFTERNOON SHADOWS filled the room when she opened her eyes, conscious of the heaviness across her middle. Half asleep, she turned to look at Russ, his face relaxed, no painful lines around his mouth. He looked much younger.

As she examined his features, he opened his eyes, surprising her with their light blue directness. "Come here," he said. It was as though he didn't remember the bad dreams.

For a moment neither of them moved; then both of them did so at the same time, reaching eagerly. Within the circle of his arms, she lay a long time until he reached to unzip her jeans.

In moments they were both undressed. The first urgency of possession was gone, and he took her leisurely, savoring her touches and exploring her body, stopping often to kiss her. As she sensed the time when he could no longer deny his body's demands, she whispered, "Love me, Russ."

Half lifting her, he slid beneath her, holding her so that he could guide himself inside. A long sigh escaped her as he filled her. His body stiffened as he tried to extend the exquisitely painful release, but her hips rotated rapidly, bringing an audible gasp from him. She collapsed on top of him, straining to get closer. He pulled her as far into him as he could, and they lay still a long time.

IT WAS ELEVEN that night when he finally left her. "If I stay tonight, you won't get any sleep, April," he told her, holding her close as he said good-night. "You have that trip tomorrow, and you need a good night's rest."

"I know," she agreed. That didn't mean she had to like letting him go. She wondered fleetingly what his parents thought of his staying away all night. *But then,* she decided, *he's a grown man. I guess he can come and go as he pleases.*

"I'll see you Tuesday when you get back," he said. "I'll call about seven, if that's okay with you." He was smoothing back her hair, lightly caressing her cheek. Her body was against his, and she pressed even closer, feeling his response.

"Yes," she said. "I'll be home by then."

"If you don't move, I might change my mind," he said, his voice deceptively quiet.

She moved back, grinning up at him. She wrinkled her nose, putting her fingers on his lips. "Call me," she said, and stepped away from him.

The room seemed much larger without his long, lanky body filling it. She took the rumpled sheets from the couch, standing for a minute looking at the bed where Russ had made out-of-this-world love to her, had carried her to an experience of loving so intense, she still burned as she thought about it.

Drawing in a shaky breath, she replaced the rumpled sheets with clean ones and got ready for bed. She set the radio clock, took Brush outside, then fed him when they came back. It wasn't quite midnight when she turned off the light. Moments later, a smile curving her lips, she imagined Russ's arms around her and went to sleep.

"WHERE WERE YOU all weekend?" Elsa asked her as she served her breakfast.

Heat filled April's face, but she took a sip of coffee to hide it from the other woman. "I was late getting in from Tahoe Saturday and was tired."

"How's the other half of the social sphere doing these days?" Elsa asked, distracted by the thought of the very rich inhabitants of the Lake Tahoe area.

"Still there," April assured her. She finished her breakfast, feeling a bit unfair at letting Elsa think she was tired when she had never felt better, except for the slight headache that came back at more frequent intervals than she cared to think about.

She had been able to ignore it all weekend, with lots of help from Russ, but it was back. Checking the rig before she climbed in with Brush, she decided she'd stop by to see Dr. Wall on her way back from Susanville.

Her thoughts went inevitably to Russ as she pulled the heavily loaded rig out onto the interstate. As early as it was and with the small amount of sleep he got over the weekend, perhaps he would still be in bed. She smiled, unashamedly wishing she were there with him.

Just out of Mineral, she passed the last real highway heading north from Route 36 and came to the curve where the truck had come head-on toward her. A wide swath was scraped along the rocky hill climbing upward from the road, and she felt a sudden chill at how easily the accident could have been tragic.

Her wheel had been fixed, and she had an appointment to have the door painted where the pickup truck had raked across her; the only time she really thought about the accident was when the pain came across her left eye. Like now. She massaged a little over the scar, and it helped, but she knew it would be back.

While the load of grain was being taken from her truck into the elevators at the loading dock, she signed for a room for the night. In the truck-stop café, she bought a drink, swallowing two aspirins in the hopes it would get rid of the pain once and for all.

It really shouldn't be bothering me this much, she thought. *But if there was a concussion, perhaps I'm still bruised up there. A good night's sleep should help.*

It did, and she felt a lot better as she headed across Stover Mountain. It could be because she was also going toward where Russ waited for her.

At the crossroads of Route 36 and Interstate 5, she turned right, following the street she had checked to find the hospital was on. She parked her rig in an unmarked area of the parking lot and went inside to look for Dr. Wall.

The receptionist who answered her question was busily filling out papers but stopped a moment to think where the doctor was at that moment.

"I'd better page him. He may be in surgery. If he is, the doctor on call for emergency will answer."

She was lucky. Dr. Wall came sauntering down the hall, pulling off his smock as he moved.

"Dr. Wall? Miss Hayden wanted to see you if you have a moment."

He stopped, looking her over, frowning. She waited, knowing he was going to remember her. Too bad she didn't have that kind of memory, but at least she recognized him.

He pointed his finger. "The truck accident?"

At her nod, he asked, "And the memory?"

"Still wherever I left it," she told him.

"Any other side effects?"

She nodded. "I've been having some pretty bad headaches. They seem to come more often."

He motioned her toward an open door. "Come in here for a moment."

She smiled apologetically. "I really didn't expect to see you; I was just hoping. I went to see Dr. Sarter in Sacramento. He removed the stitches and took X rays but didn't find anything interesting."

"Sit here," he instructed, and as she sat on the stool, he drew out a light to shine into her eyes, going from one to the other. When he finished his exploring, he sat down in front of her.

"It could be just from the bump you got. I don't see any dilation that would indicate fluid collecting from the concussion." He frowned. "But you shouldn't have bad headaches; perhaps an occasional twinge but not bad enough to bother you."

"They bother me," she said.

"Are you working now?"

"Yes."

"Go back to Dr. Sarter and get another X ray made and ask him to give me a call. Today, if you can get in there."

Agreeing to do that, she thanked him and left, glad to be heading south and slanted away from the afternoon sun. At Maxwell's she checked her rig and went directly to her car to go to the medical center. She could call Elsa later to inquire what her next schedule was. Vaguely she remembered another trip to San Diego but couldn't recall if it was tomorrow or next Wednesday.

Luck was with her at the medical center, too, and she caught Dr. Sarter before he left for the day. She explained about the headaches and about seeing Dr. Wall.

He frowned, pressing two fingers into the scar. "Does that hurt?"

"No. The pain is behind that."

"I'll get those X rays and call Dr. Wall, whatever I find, or if I don't see anything. I'd like to keep an eye on that in case there's a fluid buildup."

The same thing Dr. Wall mentioned. Well, if they were both on the lookout for the same thing, perhaps they'd know what to do if it did appear. After the X rays were taken, she walked back outside into the late-afternoon sunlight, squinting up at a cloudless blue sky.

Brush sat up as she opened the door, and she patted his wiry head as she slid behind the wheel. He had slept most of the day and was ready for a romp.

"I don't feel like playing, Brush. I'm tired." Not enough rest over the weekend, she thought, and blushed. It was a darned good reason not to rest, she decided.

In the apartment, she pushed open her one window, letting the fresh breeze blow away the musty smell. Pulling her robe from the closet, she threw her clothing into the hamper in the bathroom.

"Insurance papers," she spoke aloud. "I need to check my truck deductible and hospitalization coverage, too. Right now, before I forget."

Turning back to the closet, she reached to the top shelf to get the metal box she kept all her important papers in. Not many, but whatever she had was in there. Sitting on the floor, she opened the file and pulled out the folder that said "Insurance," flipping past the car to the truck policy. Everything was in order. She could collect some for the repairs to the truck.

Her health insurance packet was thicker, and she thumbed through several leaflets before she found the one she wanted. The medical center needed to fill those out.

Slipping the packet back behind the divider that said "Medical," she found it stuck against something and pulled it out to run her hand down to push the obstruction aside. It didn't give, and she pulled it out, an eight-by-ten brown envelope with a blue piece of paper inside.

HIS THOUGHTS on the weekend spent with April, Russ turned to face his father as he asked a question.

"How long will you be in Australia, son?"

"A year at least, but it could be as long as five. We have a contract with the government there to extract whatever minerals we can find. I understand the Snow Mountains have never been touched as far as analyzing soil to a certain depth is concerned."

"Five years?" His mother stared in consternation at him.

He laughed. "I get home leave, Mother. I won't be gone that long at any one time." He knew she was thinking that he hadn't come home very much in the past three years, claiming to be busy.

He could have come home easily, but after he'd looked for April without finding a trace and guessing she was married, he couldn't stand the thought of knowing she was happy with someone else. Especially since he'd given her up once without a second thought as to what she'd do with her life.

She belongs to me now, he thought, forgetting to follow his parents' conversation, remembering only the feel of April in his arms. *Somehow I have to convince her to go to Australia with me.*

Then you'd better make sure she knows who you are, his conscience argued patiently. *Watch your step with her, Russ, until you can find out exactly how she's going to feel once she remembers you ran off and left her because she wasn't enough woman for you.*

Dislike for the younger thoughtless Russ made him shake his head and hope he'd be given a chance to make up for some of it when he finally told April she'd once been his wife.

Chapter Twelve

Curious, she stared at the strange envelope, trying to remember what was in it. Her fingers closed over the stiff blue backing just as the phone rang.

Her heart jumped. Russ said he'd call. She let the papers slide back into the envelope, tucked them in front of the divider and pushed them down to close the box. Whatever it was, she could check it out later.

Smiling, she said into the phone, "Hello?"

"April?" The one-word question made up for the days she had been away. She could hear his deep breath, and she pressed the receiver close to her ear.

"How was the trip?" he asked.

"Unexciting."

"Suppose I come over and change the atmosphere?"

"How soon?"

"Right now."

He couldn't see her wriggle of expectancy as she said softly, "I'll be here."

"Don't move. I'll be there in half an hour."

She replaced the receiver and sat there for a moment, smiling like an idiot into space.

"It doesn't take much to make us happy, does it, Brush?" she asked the sleeping dog. "A good meal now and then and someone to love us. Very simple requirements."

As she stood up, the pain over her eye started again, and she grimaced. How long since she took the last aspirins? This was getting to be a habit.

She put off taking the aspirins until she had her shower, using a thick washcloth to hold cool water over her throbbing temple, and felt better as she dressed in a black circular skirt and white blouse, with a wide black belt cinched around her slim waist. She added the simple black sandals just as Russ knocked on the door.

He stood smiling down at her for only an instant before stepping into the room and pulling her close. He held her that way for a moment before tilting her head back to kiss her hard on the mouth.

"I missed you," he said.

"Good," she told him, putting her arm around him as they walked to the couch. Brush sat up, yawning and wagging his stubby tail by way of greeting Russ.

They sat close together, and he looked her over, his fingers tracking her lips before he touched them lightly with his. "You look tired." He frowned as he noticed the shadows under her eyes.

"Well, I am tired. I work very hard." She smiled as she said it and remembered she didn't take the aspirins. The aggravating ache was still there.

"I know," he said, and pulled her closer.

One hand rubbed up and down on her arm while his fingers played with her earlobe, sliding around to cup behind her head. He whispered, "Why do you have on so many clothes?"

Her entire body blushed. "I'm—I'm s-sorry. I thought—that is—"

He laughed, lifting his head to look down into her eyes. "Maybe you'd rather eat first."

"First?"

"Yes, first," he repeated, still smiling, and kissed her lightly this time. When she swallowed rather audibly, he asked, "Are you hungry?"

"Yes. Aren't you?"

He sighed. "Well, not exactly for food, but I guess we can wait."

"Oh."

He stood up, pulling her with him. "We wouldn't want to waste your pretty outfit." He touched the belt fastened tightly around her, emphasizing her narrow waist.

As they left the apartment, he asked, "Did you see Elsa when you came back?"

"I didn't see her today. Why?"

"I've been there a couple of times. We talked."

"Well, I hope so." She looked at him curiously. "What about?"

"She was asking about my job in Australia."

They had reached his car, and she turned to look up at him. He stared down at her without speaking, then reached around her to open the door.

A stillness filled her at the thought of his leaving for another foreign country. It would be soon, but she wasn't ready to think about it. Beneath the handbag on her lap, her fingers clasped each other tightly.

He pulled away and into light evening traffic. "Have you ever been to Australia?" she asked, more to break the silence than wanting to know.

"Yes, I was there on a trip a year ago."

He had traveled the world while she traveled up and down the state of California. True, there were a lot of miles from north to south but nothing like the thousands Russ covered each year for his company.

"Were you married while you were overseas?" she asked unexpectedly. Unexpectedly for her; she hadn't meant to ask the question.

He stiffened, and she opened her mouth to apologize, watching his mouth tighten and his hands clench on the steering wheel. After what seemed like an eternity, he said, "No, I've been divorced for several years."

She was saved from any further conversation along the lines she wished she hadn't started when he pulled into the parking lot of a restaurant. By the time he walked around to her side of the car, she had drawn a deep breath to still her uneasiness at his answer to her question. It had been, to say the least, indelicate of her.

The frown was gone from his face as she slid out to stand beside him, and he held her arm as they entered the dimly lit restaurant. A moment later they were seated, and she faced him across the table.

She picked up the wine list to study it, not seeing the names at all. Even as she sat there, she marveled at the feeling that Russ was touching her. Startled by the sensations extending into her fingers, she looked up to meet his glance.

He smiled. "This restaurant is known for its Chinese food and exotic tropical drinks."

"What do you recommend? I'm afraid my selections are limited to Elsa's daily special."

He laughed then. "Not too mean an accomplishment. Let's try one of the meals for two. How about a drink by the name of 'Lovers' Volcano'?"

"What in the world is that?"

"I have no idea. It says here it's served in a deep dish with two straws and a volcano in the center."

"An active volcano? It probably means that after you finish drinking it, you're rendered inactive."

They were still laughing when the waiter came for their orders, and she relaxed. She would be more careful what questions she asked him from now on. Perhaps, under the circumstances of having spent a weekend with her, he preferred not to think about his wife, even though they were divorced.

She looked in astonishment at the drink when it was set in front of them. It resembled a punch bowl filled with a bright pink liquid; a cluster of crushed ice in the center held a lighted candle. Two long straws were stuck into the crushed ice all the way through to the liquid.

She bent to take the straw between her lips and tasted the concoction. "Fantastic," she told him.

He sampled it and agreed. "Watch it. I'll bet it's potent."

The meal came, and she took some of everything; part of it she didn't recognize at all, but it was delicious. She sat back in the chair.

"Now I'm too full," she said.

"No," he said softly.

Across the table their glances met and locked. He reached across the table to pick up her hand. "April?"

Her lips parted. He was propositioning her right there in public, and her body answered him without hesitation. Her head no longer hurt; maybe the drink deadened it—hopefully.

He stood up, reaching for the check without relinquishing her hand. They walked to the cashier's booth hand in hand and on out to the car the same way.

He waited until she was settled in the seat before he closed the door to walk around to the driver's side. He made no move to start the car but leaned toward her. She met him halfway, lips parted to meet his kiss. Gently, he forced them farther apart and slipped his tongue inside for only an instant, withdrawing it to press hungrily against her mouth.

He raised his head, smiling, and touched her lips with two fingers before he turned back to start the car. They rode in silence to the apartment, arms around each other as they climbed the stairs.

Brush was waiting, stubby tail thumping. She took her hand away from Russ and went to open some food for the dog. As she bent to pick up his dish to give him fresh water, the pain started over her left eye.

"Darn," she muttered.

"What is it?" Russ asked from behind her.

"Oh, nothing," she said. "The drink made me a little dizzy."

As she turned around, he put his hands on her waist, looking down at her with concern. "You okay?"

She leaned against him, smiling. "Yes, I'm fine."

His hands went completely around her, locking across her back, lifting her as he bent to kiss her. Skimming her cheek, he found her mouth waiting for him.

"April, honey," he whispered. Eyes closed, she leaned into his arms, lifting her hands to lay them on each side of his face. His mouth moved on hers, tasting the sweetness she offered him.

"Can I have you, sweetheart? I need you so much." He murmured over her lips. "I haven't stopped thinking about you. I've relived the weekend so many times I've worn out my mental tapes."

Pulling away, she looked into his face. His eyes were closed tightly, squeezing the lids shut until only a dark line of lashes remained. She had seen him do that before, a sign of intense feeling within.

"What a poetic way of asking—" She stopped.

His eyes opened wide, and he laughed softly. "I thought if I were original enough, you might not argue with me."

"What makes you think I'm going to argue?"

His arms tightened briefly, then loosened as he stooped to slip his arm beneath her legs, lifting her to carry her to the couch. Instead of putting her on the couch, he knelt beside it and stretched her out on the floor, reaching to put a cushion under her head.

Without a word, he unbuttoned her blouse, removing the wide belt. He unzipped the skirt, sliding it over her hips as she lifted them. His breath was coming quickly as he lay beside her, pulling her into his arms.

Reaching for him, she brought his face to hers, running her tongue lightly across his chin, along his jaw, to his ear. The tip of the moist instrument went inside to caress the sensitive rim, and he moaned softly in response.

Gently, he turned her on her back and finished undressing her, kissing between the small breasts, circling them with a light row of flicks from his tongue. She murmured his name, and her body twisted toward him.

Together they managed to get his clothing off, and he knelt over her. Her legs were drawn up halfway, and he stretched them out, his long fingers sliding from her knees down the calf of her legs to her ankles. He rubbed the bottom of her foot, bringing it up to kiss it, touching between her toes with his tongue.

She tried to pull away, but he held on, massaging from her toes to her ankles, flicking his tongue along the inside flesh of her leg to her thighs. She lay still, no longer trying to get away from him, waiting to see where he would go next with his kisses.

His touches were ones she had never experienced, and she lay in the warmth of her desire for him, in the heat of her need. Her eyes were wide open, but she saw nothing. She felt everything. Her hands fluttered toward him, but she let them drop beside her as he drained away her strength.

She cried out as her body dissolved in the rushing tumult he created, holding her suspended as wave after wave of liquid heat built to a crescendo, lavishing them with a torrent of her love for him.

Her breath came in soft sobs as he lowered himself, easing into her. He lay still, waiting. Her head moved back and forth, and he bent to kiss her, catching her parted lips beneath his. The circles beneath her closed eyes were moist.

She opened her eyes, staring up into his face, and he smiled. "Sweetheart?"

Her arms came around him with a quick movement, and she held on to him as he began his strokes.

"Oh, Russ. Oh, darling." Her words drifted to a whisper as he kissed her, as he caressed her within and without, as he took them both through the culmination of their love.

And finally they lay clasped in each other's arms.

Slowly, she came back into consciousness, fully aware of her body, of every pore of her skin that had tasted of Russ's love, every nerve end opened to the passion he roused in her. He knew the desire was there, and he had taken her through the enchantment of releasing that desire with the torrent of love for him. She shivered, but she wasn't cold. It was the flames still enveloping her, fires glowing inside as she lay in his arms.

His whisper was against her ear. "Are you cold?"

She snuggled closer. "No."

He held her a moment longer, then said, "We'd better cover you, honey."

Reluctant to let him move away from her, she nodded, slowly letting her hands slide from around him. Light fingers touched her closed eyes, the damp circles underneath them.

"You're so lovely, April." His voice barely audible, he went on as she opened her eyes to look straight into his light blue ones. "You're so sweet, and you know how to give me that sweetness. I—" He stopped, the old look of pain showing in his eyes before he closed them tightly. He kissed her nose, lifting his head again to open his eyes and smile down at her.

"Stay here," he told her, and sat up away from her.

Her outstretched hand, trying to hold him, dropped back to her side as she watched him gently urge Brush off the couch as he opened it. He remembered the steps required to fix the couch into a bed, spreading sheets and a blanket, before he came back to stand over her.

She looked up at him, the long body, gangly arms out from his body as he bent to lift her. The old look of familiarity came back, faintly reminding her of someone. But there was no one else. She closed her eyes as a tiny pain started over the left one.

The bed gave beneath them as he lay beside her, pulling the blanket up, tucking it beneath her arms, covering her breasts after he caressed the dark tips with the ends of his fingers. The tips grew rigid, and his eyes lingered on the firm mounds before he let the cover drop over them. His eyes came back to her lips, upward, to meet her dark gaze.

"How do you feel?" he asked.

"Wonderful." She turned to face him, moving her body until it fitted its curves to the hardness of his. One arm went around him, and her fingers splayed across the hard muscles of his shoulders. She dug into the firm flesh.

Beneath her touch, his body went rigid, his breathing becoming rapid and deep. Her hand moved with tantalizing slowness down over his hips. A slight covering of wiry hair tingled her palms as her fingers explored hard angles of his body, pressing into the familiar firm flesh.

His hands found the responsive parts of her body, almost roughly pulling her between his thighs. He held her away from him while his hands reached back of her, coming immediately back to movement between them. She waited, gasping softly as his hand eased her legs apart.

"Help me, April," he begged.

She lifted her leg to slide it across him, arching her hips toward him, and he filled her very being with the measured movement of his hard body. For a timeless moment he lay within her, a moment filled with twin realizations of wanting each other, of knowing that wanting would be satisfied. They held the moment, waiting to savor the fulfillment, knowing they would give themselves completely to each other.

His kisses began at the tiny little ache over her eye, as though he knew it hurt, light kisses, trailing across her nose, touching her lips. Her own lips parted, wanting his mouth to linger, but he moved on over her chin, around her jawline to the throbbing pulse in her throat. Their bodies remained quiet as he kissed upward over her ear to her temple, coming back to touch her closed eyes.

She tried not to hurry him, but she had no control over the convulsive jerk of her body as he once more found her waiting lips. Parted, they accepted his experimental touch of the tip of his tongue across the edge of her teeth.

The groan wrung from deep inside him came a split second ahead of his thrusting tongue demanding access to the warm moistness of her mouth, his plunging body demanding a response she had been waiting to give. Beneath him, her body writhed with liquid strength, taking the love he offered, returning it in full.

"I don't want to—" he whispered, but there was no holding back as they were lifted together, the violent release bringing a gasping outcry from him as a long, shuddering sigh escaped her parted lips.

She knew when he left her, knew when he returned, felt the warmth as he pulled the blanket over her. Her pliant body rolled slightly to be close to him, and his arms once again surrounded her.

"April?"

She didn't want to talk; she wanted to sleep wrapped around his body. Her fingers found his lips to press against them, to make him go to sleep with her. If she slept, the pain would surely go away without her taking any more aspirins.

"No," she said, "I want to sleep."

His soft laughter vibrated through his chest where her breasts lay. "I might let you sleep after a while, but right now I think we should talk."

Reluctantly, she moved her head back to look at him. He had turned out the light, and all she could see were blurred outlines of his features.

"Are you going to explain?" she asked.

His sudden stiffening surprised her. As his arms tightened, he asked, "Explain what?"

"I—Russ, I know I'm twenty-seven." She hesitated. "I know I'm old enough to—to—" She stopped, then blurted out, "No one has ever made love to me like that. I haven't—haven't had a lot of experience."

"Can't you remember?"

She sighed against his throat as she nestled close once more. "I want to, Russ, but I can't. I see shadows, but they keep moving away from me."

"April? We have to get married," he said quietly.

Unsure if she had heard him right, she stayed where she was, but her eyes opened wide, seeing nothing with her face resting on his chest.

"Did you hear me?"

"Yes. Yes, Russ, I heard you." Held in his unrelenting embrace, she waited. When he remained silent, she asked, "Have to get married? I'm not pregnant."

"I know that, honey. I made sure of it." He kissed the top of her head, and his fingers came up to tangle in the thickness of her hair. "That isn't the only reason people have to get married."

"Then why?" she insisted.

"I can't leave you behind when I go to Australia. You have to go with me." He pushed her away from him, holding her chin firmly with thumb and forefinger. She strained to see his expression. The lightness of his eyes was barely visible, and she could see the movement of his lips as he spoke. "You could go with me without getting married if you prefer, but I think we should get married."

Lord knows she wanted to say yes. "I don't even know who I am, Russ. I can't marry you like this."

"I know who you are, April. You're all I'll ever want. In case you haven't guessed by now, I love you very much."

Struggling to sit up away from him, she reached across to turn on the lamp at the end of the couch. He sat up with her, pulling her back into his arms as she faced him.

"How can you know that in such a short time? We've only known each other a couple of weeks."

"Do you love me?" he asked, watching her closely, reading the answer in her eyes before she told him.

Her fingers went up to rub across the almost-invisible scar at the edge of her eyebrow. The puzzled expression remained in her dark eyes as they went over his face, coming back to meet his smile.

"I love you, Russ, but—"

"We'll take you back to the doctor. If he can't find anything, perhaps he'll recommend a specialist that we can see. Sometimes just the right question triggers a memory." For a moment the lines appeared around his mouth, quickly disappearing as she touched them.

"How long before you have to leave?"

"About ten days, but I'm sure I can get an extension for such an important reason." He smiled as he caught her chin again to force her to look at him. "Will you marry me?"

As she hesitated, the smile left his face, and he said urgently, "I can understand how you feel, April, but we love each other. I can't go without you."

The pain darted through her eye, and the hazy outline she tried to bring into focus slipped away from her. Russ held her chin, his mouth only a breath away from hers. Leaning toward him, she touched his mouth with hers.

"Maybe a specialist will help. If he says it will be years before I remember who I am, then you'll have a bride with an unknown past."

Russ slid down beneath the blanket, easing her with him, and once more their bodies fit together. There was no longer a demand for satisfaction; they were content. He leaned across her, and the light went out.

"You sound so tired, honey. I should have known better than to stay with you tonight, but I couldn't help it." He kissed her cheek, stroking her bare hip with light fingertips.

"It's heaven to be in your arms, Russ. I may be tired, but don't blame yourself. Hold me, that's all I want."

Chapter Thirteen

The playful tugging at the blanket woke her, and she looked into Brush's button eyes. Her attempt to reach to pull the blanket away from him was blocked by a big hand weighing her arm down. Her body was curved against Russ, still sleeping, his breath warm against her cheek.

"Hello, darling." His husky whisper sent a thrill from the warm spot his breath touched to the tip of her toes, and she wriggled them rapturously.

The hand across her dropped to lie on her breast, his fingers drifting back and forth until the creamy brown tip hardened.

"Brush wants to go outside," she said.

He moaned his protest but whispered, "That's the safest thing for me to do right now. Don't go away."

Her smile followed his movements as he slipped his pants on with only a T-shirt and went toward the door. Brush dropped his hold on the blanket to follow him, his stubby tail wagging happily.

As the door closed behind them, she slipped from the bed and went into the bathroom. Reaching quickly for the aspirin bottle, she took two. She splashed water on her face and brushed her teeth, wrapping a towel around her as she walked back into the room.

Her robe lay on the floor by the couch where they had discarded it the night before. Against the wall was the metal box with her insurance papers.

I'd better get that back in the proper place, she thought. *Next time I need it, I'll wonder what happened to it.* She picked up the box, thinking briefly of the blue paper, but she put it on the shelf as she heard Russ and Brush returning.

At their hurried entrance, she turned to smile at them. Russ shook his head, brushing his hand through his hair.

"It's pouring rain. Do you have a schedule?"

"No, thank goodness. I don't mind the rain, but Stover Mountain is slow going when it's wet."

He was standing in front of her, his hands playing with the knot she had looped to fasten the towel around her. "When is your next scheduled run?"

"Tomorrow." She took one step closer to him, lifting her head to meet his smiling glance.

"Do you want to postpone it to see that specialist? We could get the marriage license, too."

She shook her head and wished she hadn't. The tiny ache was back behind her left eye. "I don't want to put off this run. It's medical supplies to the distribution point, and they have to be delivered to several places. They're low because of the strike last month at the plant where I pick them up."

"Where to?"

"Susanville."

He frowned. "That means overnight."

"I know." His hands continued to fasten and unfasten the towel ends, and finally he let it drop to the floor.

He pulled her up to him, his hands clasping beneath her buttocks. His mouth was damp and cool on hers. The pressure increased, and his teeth sank into her soft lips. Her tongue pushed against them, and he freed her lips to tease her tongue, biting, then slowly drawing it inside his mouth.

He forced her body closer to him, his desire for her outlined hard against her pelvic bones. Gradually, he released his hold on her, letting his hands slide upward to curve over her hips.

"Later, darling," he whispered, making small kisses on her forehead. "Get dressed and let's go get some breakfast."

As she took jeans and a pale yellow shirt from the closet, Russ put fresh water and some dry food into Brush's dish. She stepped into the bathroom to brush her hair, taking a second to look at her paleness and adding a touch of color to her cheeks and lips. The yellow shirt was trimmed in piping along the western-style yoke that came to a point just over the small imprint made by her breasts. Tight jeans outlined the slender curves, still feeling the touch of his hands on them.

Russ folded the sheets and blanket, making their bed back into its couch form. He had put on the shirt he had worn the night before and was standing with his back to her, buttoning it and tucking it into his pants.

Her bag lay on the lamp table, and she reached to pick it up, checking to see she had placed her keys in the outside pocket.

He turned, his eyes taking in the trim figure in front of him, and bent to kiss her.

"Ready?" he asked. For a moment she thought she saw the odd sadness reflected in his eyes, but he smiled down at her, and she forgot about it.

Brush sat up expectedly, and she said, "I suppose you can come. We won't be gone long, will we?"

"He can go with us, sure." Russ opened the door, waiting for her to scoop the little dog up into her arms. He closed the door behind them and slipped his arm around her as they walked down the steps.

The car was pulled close enough that she didn't get too wet as he opened the door, and she tumbled in holding Brush to her chest. Laughing, she put him in the back seat, looking at Russ as he slid hurriedly in beside her.

"What's funny?" he asked.

"Brush. He's so happy to go with us, you'd think he was never allowed out of the house."

"Which reminds me, I'll have to check on the quarantine regulations into Australia."

"What do you mean?"

"Regulations for animals going to foreign countries differ with the country, so I have to check to see what Australia's requirements are as pertains to Brush."

"Oh." She hadn't thought that far ahead, not quite sure the marriage proposal hadn't been a dream. A quiet thrill started in the vicinity of her heart and slid down her body to her thighs. Just being held in his arms, having him make love to her—that was paradise beyond all her fantasies. Being married to Russ— She glanced at him to meet the light blue gaze and smiled. Her hand reached for his, and he took it from the wheel to squeeze her fingers.

"What are you thinking about?" he asked.

"Brush, of course," she said, laughing again.

"Liar," he said softly. "You're thinking about last night and this morning and last weekend."

"Yes," she agreed, and they both fell silent. She hadn't considered marriage to Russ. His leave was almost up; he never mentioned his job or the kidnapping experience. It seemed so long ago, but the tension in him at times, the unhappiness in his face, the lines around his mouth, all attested to the fact that he had not forgotten.

"April?"

Looking up, she saw he had stopped at a small coffee shop and had spoken to her. Deep in her thoughts, she hadn't heard.

"Want to make a run for it?" he asked.

Rain came down in a steady downpour, but they were close to the entrance. "Sure," she said, and not waiting for him to come to open the door on her side, she was out and running with him as he came around the car. Standing beneath the overhang, he took her coat from around her and shook it before they entered the restaurant.

"Now, about my proposal."

Startled, she looked up at him after they gave their breakfast orders. "What about it?"

"You don't sound too enthusiastic."

She rubbed her eye. "It doesn't seem real, Russ. I've known you such a short time. I know I want to marry you, but is this really the way things are done?"

"I don't know," he said simply. "It's been a long time for me, and I had known her since she was very young. Our families took care of everything." He watched her, seeing the uncertainty in her face.

"Where is she now?" she asked.

"April." His mouth worked, but he stared at her without adding any more. Just her name. "There's so much I need to say, and I don't know how to say it." He took a deep breath.

"You don't have to tell me anything, Russ, if it's painful. Don't talk about it if it hurts," she said.

"Yes, it hurts," he said simply. "It hurts like hell to think about her."

His quiet statement jolted through her, stilling her heartbeat for one second; then it started a furiously protesting thud. *You can't hurt from one love and take on another,* she thought, watching him.

"If that's true, Russ, I can't marry you. You still love her." An unexpected pain tightened her chest as she leaned toward him. "I have no memory at all, and you have too much." She shook her head. "We couldn't survive that way."

"I love you, April." He sat back in the booth. "Let me work out the rest of it, but that much you can bet your life on."

He stopped as their breakfast arrived and without looking at it, went on. "Will you go with me to meet my parents?"

Parents, a marriage proposal, meet the family, move to a foreign country.

I have to remember, she told herself. *I have to remember that love is what counts and that Russ loves me. I love Russ.* The flames he fanned to an intensely burning fire inside her couldn't be done by anyone but Russ; she knew that for sure. In ten days, perhaps something would happen to bring her past up-to-date.

She looked across at him, smiling. "Suppose you find out I'm a woman with a past, Russ? What would you tell your parents then?"

The pain was there, shouting for recognition, but he hid it behind a smile. "I'll take that chance. Will you go with me to meet them after we leave here?"

"Yes." She wiped her mouth, feeling better the moment she agreed to go with him.

THE RAIN HAD STOPPED as they approached the small town of Brookeville where the Calloways lived. A typical country town of farmers, grape vineyards and orchards.

"I'm not sure I'm ready for this, Russ. I feel like I'm eighteen and scared to death."

"They're ordinary people, April. Don't be frightened." He smiled, but she noticed the lines deepening around his mouth. He wasn't so sure, either, she decided.

His hand on her elbow gave her a needed touch as they walked up the sidewalk across a cracked piece of cement at the steps. The door opened, and a man stood waiting for them.

"Good morning, Dad," Russ said, smiling at him. He turned to look down at her, his gaze softening as he took in the wide dark eyes and the lower lip pulled nervously between her teeth.

She swallowed, holding out her hand. "Hello, Mr. Calloway."

He ran his hand through the thinning white hair, his dark eyes going from Russ to April. He shook her hand, motioning them inside.

"Russ has talked about you, April," he said. "Come in and meet my wife." He knew about her, but he was uneasy.

Mrs. Calloway stood just inside the living-room door as they turned from the entrance hallway. She was a small woman, her gray hair drawn back in an old-fashioned bun. Light blue eyes, like her son's, were faded from the years. They met April's dark ones and looked back at Russ.

"Mother, this is April."

Her mouth felt stretched out of shape as she gave her a tentative smile. Mrs. Calloway didn't think much of her son's bringing a strange woman into their house early on a rainy morning, a woman they were well aware he had slept with the night before.

The awkward silence was broken by Mrs. Calloway's offer of coffee, and she followed Russ's motion to sit on the couch as they waited.

"I understand you were in an accident and can't remember anything, April," Mr. Calloway said. He was standing by the mantel in front of a picture of Russ posed by a big jet, briefcase in hand.

She wet her lips. "Yes." Glancing at Russ, she went on. "I'm thinking about seeing a specialist. I was hoping I'd remember on my own, but it's been a long time."

He nodded, his eyes going over her. Mrs. Calloway returned with coffee on a tray, and he turned to help her pour and pass the cups to them. She gave her attention to her coffee, smiling as Russ poured milk into hers. He winked at her and sat down beside her, facing his parents.

"I've asked April to marry me. She said yes," he said quietly.

His parents stared at them, consternation plainly visible in their faces. His mother's mouth worked, and she set her cup of coffee down with a clatter. His father stood stiffly by her side.

Russ nodded as if they'd spoken. "Yes, I know what you're thinking, but we love each other and don't want to wait on the off chance she'll regain her memory right away. I'm taking her to Australia with me."

April watched the scene as she might a movie of intrigue, wondering what was going on in the minds of the two people they faced. Clearly they disapproved. It didn't matter to Russ. He was old enough to make decisions without asking his parents, but he had wanted them to know what he planned.

She didn't absorb much of what went on as she listened to Russ explain what he was going to do—that as soon as she returned from her next trip, they would be married.

"Are you still driving that rig?" Mr. Calloway asked, turning to April. "I'm surprised doctors will let you go back on the road."

She put her cup down on the table in front of her. "That's one of the odd things about my partial amnesia, Mr. Calloway. I remember my job; I've had no trouble handling the rig; I remember all the places I've been, where I live. I just don't remember any people."

For the first time she realized the strangeness of that facet of her amnesia; she remembered things and places but not people. How peculiar, she thought, as she watched the play of expression over the faces of the people nearby. They, too, thought it was strange and looked doubtful.

Well, she thought in their defense, *I'm marrying their son; they have a right to be curious about the woman who'll be their daughter-in-law.*

When Russ stood up and reached for her hand, she was glad. She was glad to get outside of the house, out of the formal living room with two pictures of Russ on the mantel, both evidently taken in the past few years. Where were all the family pictures people displayed on such a large mantel?

And then it hit her. She had no pictures in her small apartment, either. But Russ told her she was an only child. Why didn't the Calloways talk about her parents? Maybe they thought it would bother her, but she would have loved to have talked about them with neighbors. Russ had been gone for years, but the Calloways had lived in the same house all their lives.

More or less collapsing into the seat as Russ helped her into the car, she stared in surprise at her shaking hands.

I'm a grown woman, she thought, frowning. *Why am I so upset over meeting Russ's family?* It didn't stop her shaking. A big hand reached over to cover hers, clasped painfully together in her lap, and she turned a questioning look at Russ.

"It's all right, honey." Behind the tanned skin she saw his paleness. The lines around his mouth were drawn tightly even as he smiled reassuringly at her.

"They don't like me," she told him.

He shook his head. "They're uneasy about your amnesia, April, thinking it may be permanent after all this time."

"What if it is?" she asked.

His grip tightened on her hands. "No, darling. There's the chance it might, but don't you believe it."

"I didn't think too much about it until now. Until we talked about getting married, there was no one else it could matter to. Now there's you, Russ, and I'm almost afraid. And your parents—"

"I'm thirty-one years old, April. You don't think I brought you here to ask permission to marry, do you? It was on the off chance that seeing Mother and Dad would prompt a memory. It didn't, but it doesn't mean I give up on your getting your memory back."

He wanted her to believe, but he had his uncertainties, too. They had one chance left—a specialist. The darkness of her unknown past already cast a shadow on their future.

Brush, ignored long enough, jumped between them, wriggling. Absently, she petted his rough coat, her eyes still meeting the warmth of Russ's gaze. He leaned across the small dog to kiss her cheek, turning to start the car.

They rode in silence toward her apartment. "What time does the medical center open?" he asked.

"Why?"

"We're going there today and talk to Dr. Sarter."

"The center's closed on Wednesday," she told him after a moment. "Dr. Sarter operates a Children's Hospital all day today, and they have an intern for emergencies. I don't want to talk to anyone but him."

"I can understand that, April, but you'll be gone until Friday night if you take that run."

"Another couple of days won't matter one way or the other," she told him.

"I'm going with you on the run to Susanville," he said.

She laughed. "No, Russ. As you say, I'm over eighteen. The California Highways Commission doesn't allow me to take anyone not insured in my rig, and my insurance doesn't cover you."

"I don't care about insurance."

"They could take my license, Russ. I care, and you can't go with me."

They were stopped at her apartment, and he came around to open the door for her. Brush hopped over her to the ground, racing for his favorite strip of grass. She slid out to stand near him as they waited.

"Do you think you'll be this stubborn when your memory returns?" he asked, smiling down at her.

"Perhaps worse," she said, her head tilted back to look up at him. The warm, moist wind stirred her hair, and he put his hand up to brush it away from her cheek as he bent to kiss her.

He sighed. "If you have a temper to match, I'm in trouble," he said, taking her arm as Brush scampered back to join them.

Inside the room, they stood looking around at the few reminders of her life before Russ. After a moment he pulled her around and against his chest, holding her close as his hands came up to tangle in her damp hair.

Her mouth was ready for him as he tilted her chin. The lazy exploration of his lips over hers took only a moment to quicken her breath and reawaken the quiescent passion between them. She was aware of his body's response as he slid one hand behind her hips, holding them together.

He murmured a question against her mouth, and her body melted in liquid surrender as he picked her up to carry her to the couch.

"Why didn't we go to a motel with a king-sized water bed?" he moaned against her throat. "This thing is a lot of trouble."

"But worth it?" she asked, hands busy with his shirt.

"Yes, darling," he agreed, cooperating with her, removing their clothing. As their bodies blended eagerly together, the couch, the room, the amnesia—everything receded before the onrushing impatience of their desire for each other.

Chapter Fourteen

She ate breakfast at Maxwell's, checking the posted schedules. On Monday she was due for a San Bernardino run, but she'd have to cancel if she did as Russ suggested and went back to see Dr. Sarter.

I'd better go, she thought, rubbing the familiar spot over her left eye. *At least to get something stronger than aspirin for this pain.*

Elsa came around the counter and stopped in front of her. "Where you been? Are you okay?"

"I stayed in out of the rain. Aside from a headache now and then, I feel fine." Her whole body blushed beneath the cotton of her shirt and the faded blue jeans. Very okay, she wanted to assure Elsa. Instead, she asked, "Do you think Wade would take my run Monday if he's in? I need to see the doctor again and am scheduled for San Bernardino."

"I'll ask him this afternoon. He's due back, and if I don't see you, I'll tack his answer up on the board."

"Thanks, Elsa," she said, paying for her breakfast and waving a general hand in the direction of the other diners in the room.

Outside, she walked around her truck, Brush ahead of her, sniffing his usual route. The body shop had done a good job on the paint repair, and she now sported a solid-colored royal blue door rather than blue with a swath of silver metal showing where the pickup had plowed along the side.

"Freak accidents cause more damage than ones we could even plan, Brush, if there's ever any laid out according to plan," she told the small dog as she followed him up on the high seat of the truck. "At least just my head was hurt; not much damage to the vehicle's body, nor mine." She pulled the truck out of the parking lot and turned down the familiar street leading to Interstate 5.

Her thoughts went to Russ, and she smiled, her lips parting as she recalled his arms around her. *Lord, how can you love someone so much after such a short time?* Even with misgivings about her temporary amnesia, she couldn't imagine letting Russ go to Australia without her.

The rain of the day before had lingered off and on during the night, and a mist of fog was beginning to burn off as she turned east at Red Bluff. Traffic was picking up over the mountain with the improving weather, and motor homes moved in both directions.

Workers were waiting for her as she pulled in with the needed medical supplies that had been delayed by the strike. In record time the truck was empty, and she looked at her watch. It was early; she could make the return trip today.

No, I can't, she decided. She was tired, and her eyes ached from squinting against the almost-constant pain behind them. Driving into the late-afternoon sun would not help the situation. She signed in for the night and went to bed.

If Russ were anywhere but his parents, she thought, *I'd call him. I need to just talk.* But he was there, and her misgivings about the Calloways' feelings where she was concerned surfaced again.

They don't know me well enough to dislike me, she argued silently as she stared into the darkness. *They should be glad for Russ.* Or perhaps they remembered his first marriage, when he was too young, but that was years ago. He was old enough now to know what he wanted. Twisting and turning, she finally slept.

As soon as she opened her eyes the next morning, she wondered what day it was, lying there until she figured out that it was now Friday. The thought of getting back to Russ was the only thing that got her out of bed. Would he be able to get the marriage license? What other arrangements would have to be made in the short time remaining before he was due to leave for Australia?

Without eating breakfast, she started back across Stover Mountain. By the time she reached Red Bluff, she was hungry enough to eat, slightly nauseous from the headache and emptiness in her stomach. Stopping at a familiar truck stop, she had a sandwich and carbonated drink filled with lots of ice and was feeling a little steadier as she headed south toward home.

Inside the apartment, she opened her window to the afternoon breeze and gave Brush fresh water and food. Standing by the sink, she stared thoughtfully at the counter, trying to remember what she had done with the insurance papers. They needed to be turned in; plus, if she saw a specialist, other forms would have to be filled out.

I'm having a hard time recalling anything, she thought, frowning in concentration. *Not only what happened a month ago but what happened yesterday. Well, I haven't forgotten everything,* she corrected herself, smiling. Russ. She remembered everything about him and his arms around her.

Checking the shelves and top of the small chest in quest of the insurance papers, she gave up and went back to the closet, reaching upward for the metal box. They were probably back in there, the last place she had put them.

Sitting on the floor, her back against the couch, she flipped the top of the fireproof box, pulling the dividers forward to the one marked "Insurance."

"Ah," she said to the dog beside her. "Just where I put them." Pulling them out, she flipped to see if they were all in order, found they were and laid them beside her as she closed the top.

The paper that caught under the lid was blue, and she poked it down with her finger, then opened the box again to pull the paper out. It was the one she questioned a few days before, but Russ had interrupted her, and she forgot about it.

The blue part was stiff backing behind a formal-looking document typed double-spaced. Puzzled, she stared.

Divorce decree. *What in the world am I doing with someone's divorce papers?* She read the entire page, then reread it. Her world upended, crashing around her into splintering silence as she digested the words in front of her.

Russell Calloway had been her husband. She was April Hayden Calloway, divorced six years ago on the grounds of incompatibility. Incompatibility? What did that mean? A red haze came between her and the wavering print. Blinding reality struck a numbing blow to her midsection.

Russ divorced her, but he came back to make love to her. She was an easy mark. She didn't know who she was, but Russ knew. He knew how to make love to her; knew how to make her love him; respond to his tenderness, his caring; knew she would never suspect he was her husband who had left her six years ago.

"We were too young," he said. Six years ago she was twenty-one; Russ, four years older. She had been married when she was eighteen and Russ was twenty-two. Too young. But how? What about a twenty-seven-year-old April Hayden?

He was planning to marry her again. She was old enough now; old enough to—

The pain over her eye started again as she sat there, the hurt inside her too much to accept. Why? Why?

The room grew dark, and still she sat there. The phone rang, but she didn't move. There was a thundering noise at the door, and still she sat there. Someone called her name, demanding an answer that she made no attempt to give. Brush sat in front of her to get her attention, but she didn't stir.

The pain over her eye grew to a biting sharpness, and she knew she should get up and take some aspirins. Vaguely, she wondered if the knocking was at her door, deciding that it couldn't be. Russ would be over later, but wasn't it too early for him?

Her husband, Russ Calloway. *Then we don't have to get married.* A dim thought came forward; *I'm already his wife. Can't we just go on to Australia without getting married again?*

The papers rustled in her fingers, and she stared at the faint outline in the darkness. The noise had stopped, but she became aware of a rattle of a key in the door, the sound of it being shoved inward.

"April?" a familiar voice called. "April, what the hell—?"

The light came on, and she blinked up at the tall man standing there, long arms at an angle to his sides. He was on his knees beside her, holding her.

"Honey? What happened? What—?"

Russell Calloway. She remembered now—the long arms dangling at his sides as he told her he was leaving. A much younger Russell Calloway telling a much younger April Calloway she wasn't enough woman for him, telling her she smothered him, tied him down to an immature wife when he needed more experience.

"I feel like I've raised you from a baby," she recalled his saying as though he had just spoken. But the Russell Calloway leaning over her had lines etched around his mouth, eyes filled with pain. He begged her to answer him.

She watched him curiously as her memory returned by degrees and with a vengeance she thought unnecessary, the memory that deserted her long enough for Russ to make a complete fool of her, so that he could come home to see if she was any more a woman now than she was six years ago.

Into the present came the memory of the terrorists: the days of anguish as she waited and watched to hear he was safe; the visit to the Calloways; the accusations from his mother that she was responsible for Russ being in danger.

All those years they hadn't cared enough to check on her, never realized how sick she was, never called.

Russ sent money, money that was supposed to make up for his deserting her, specifically for the education he wanted her to complete. She had used it to start her own trucking business.

The education she had always thought important ceased to have any meaning after Russ left her. What she needed was something to take up her time, something to keep her busy so she wouldn't have to think of the husband who left her in search of maturity, something lacking in the teenager he married just out of high school.

Her business prospered; she hadn't done bad at all. Nor had Russ, a chemical engineer with a big firm, free to find all the women who could teach him more than she could.

In answer to his repeated questions, she finally said, "I'm all right, Russ. There's nothing wrong with me."

He gathered her to him, patting her shoulder, murmuring to her. "My God, honey. When you didn't answer the phone or my knocking, I couldn't imagine where you were. Your car's outside, so I went to the manager of the building to get a key."

She struggled away from him, trying to sit up. "No," he said, "let me help you."

He lifted her and put her on the couch, sitting close to her. He brushed her hair back. "Darling, did something happen on your trip? Why didn't you call me when you got in?"

"Nothing happened on the trip." Her voice was flat.

She didn't look at him, her eyes fastened to the pages lying beside the overturned metal box that held all her important papers. Including her divorce papers from Russell Calloway.

She moaned, burying her head in her hands, rocking back and forth, remembering. Nausea boiled up inside, threatening to gag her.

"Don't, April." He put his arms around her, but she was up and away from him, brushing his hands aside.

The pain was gone from over her left eye, but the pain scorching through her now was worse. No aspirins would ease that pain, not even for a few moments.

"We'd better get you to a doctor," he said, coming toward her.

"I don't need a doctor, Russ. The two I saw the first of this week said I shouldn't keep having headaches."

"You didn't tell me you were having headaches. You haven't mentioned it to me. How long has this been going on?"

"It doesn't matter," she said.

He started toward her again. "Of course it matters. You have to check on those things, especially after a concussion."

"I don't have them anymore."

"What? You just said—"

"All I needed was to open Pandora's box." She turned away from him and went to the sink to run water into a glass, drinking it all before she looked around at him.

"April, what—?"

She looked at him, the stranger that wasn't a stranger. Long ago he had been the only man to ever make love to her; today he was the same man—the only one to ever make love to her. *I can't stand this pain,* she thought.

"See the papers on the floor, Russ?" she asked, pointing a shaking finger.

He looked at the papers scattered there, then back at her. "What's that got to do with your headache?"

"Pick them up and look at them," she told him.

One more look at her face and he picked up the blue-backed papers, turning them over to read the print on the front.

His body went stiff as he read, and she watched with the same curious detachment as the color drained from his face. His hands clenched, crumpling the legal papers that had ended their marriage six years ago.

Slowly, he raised his head to meet her condemning eyes. The pain she had wondered about was there—white lines enclosing the firm mouth that had taken her to the ultimate high of complete love. His hands, now crumpling the papers, had held her, caressing her, teaching her what he had learned from other, more experienced women.

"I tried to tell you, April. I wanted to explain about how wrong I was to leave you, that I've hurt as much as you over the years." He shook his head, looking down at the papers in his hand. "I only tried once to get in touch with you, it's true, but Mother and Dad didn't know anything about you, and I couldn't find out. My letter came back. I thought you had remarried."

"Your parents, Russ?" Her laugh almost strangled her over the threatening nausea. "I felt sorry for them when you were kidnapped. I went to see them, Russ, and did they tell you what happened?" The picture of the house where the Calloways lived came in front of her: the broken piece of cement on the walk, the uncarpeted hallway, the mantel with only one picture.

"They said *I* was the cause of your being held by terrorists. *I* deserted you." Her face twisted with the indescribable destruction crumbling her insides. Her indrawn breath ended on a strangled sob. "You play dirty, Russ," she whispered over the pain. "Why did you plan to marry me, knowing eventually I'd remember?"

He stood there, long arms dangling as she had seen them recently, always reminding her of someone long ago and the day he told her he was leaving. She remembered every move he made that day as he argued his side of a marriage between two people too young to know any better. April knew she loved Russ, and for her that had been enough. But not for Russ.

"You made my love cheap, Russ. You made it obscene." Her voice was entirely without expression as she went on. "You turned my love into something vulgar and indecent." Bracing herself against the counter, hands flat on the rim of the stainless-steel sink, she faced him with brooding eyes, dark with the ache deep inside her.

They stared at each other, and suddenly she couldn't resist shoving the knife just a little deeper into her own soul. "Did I grow up, Russ? Does my love satisfy you a little more now than when I was twenty-one?"

He didn't answer, and she went on. "I haven't tied you down yet with immature emotions, but it would happen sooner or later." Her eyes narrowed against the pain as she added softly, "No. Leave now, Russ. Get out of this room. Don't take unnecessary chances on being unable to get the fulfillment you need." Her eyes flashed as her head came up and her words came through clenched teeth. "Get out!"

"You must listen to me, honey. I know how you feel—"

"Do you? Do you, now?" She took a step toward him. "I waited for you to come back to me, Russ. We loved each other, so how could you not finally realize you couldn't live without me any more than I could you? Of course you'd come back. And I'd take you back even after you found someone who knew the ropes to satisfy your manly desires. But you didn't come back, Russ."

He tried to stop her, but she was reliving the abyss of despair she endured when she knew he wouldn't be back. Ever.

"I went to pieces, Russ. I spent ten days in the hospital while they treated physical symptoms of dehydration and a virus they couldn't identify. Then I went to a psychiatrist who was warm and gentle and fatherly."

He took a step toward her, but she shook her head, her eyes daring him to touch her. "But I survived. Oh, yes, I survived. No thanks to you or your parents." Her voice went flat, losing the hostility. "I should thank you for the money. It put me where I am today, with a lot of hard work on my part."

She was wrung out. Perspiration dripped down her face, and she wiped it away. On shaky legs, she moved away from the sink, past him, into the bathroom, closing the door behind her, locking it.

She splashed cold water in her face and over her arms, but it was no use. Bending over the commode, she gave in to the heaving inside of her, retching until her body strained against her empty stomach.

Weakly, she leaned against the sink. She held a wet cloth to her face and throat, finally rinsing her mouth and brushing her teeth.

"Are you all right, April?"

All right? How can you be all right when the world split into pieces and you're drifting away from everything you ever loved? When you know you've been betrayed by the only one you'll ever love and everything in you protests it can't be true—but it is.

Closing her eyes, she stood still for a long moment. "Yes. I'm all right," she said quietly. "Don't worry about me, Russ. I'll be fine. Just go—just go away." Her teeth began to chatter, and she clamped them together.

"I want to explain, April. I know it's hard for you to understand, but let me try." His voice was pleading with her.

"I understand. It's simple enough that even I understand." She unlocked the door and walked back to face him.

His gaze went over her white face, lavender circles under her eyes. Dark hair had pulled loose from the clamp holding it back over her ears and clung damply to her cheek. Her skin shone with a film of moisture.

"I can't leave you like this," he said.

She smiled. "You've left me in worse shape, Russ. At least I'm old enough to handle this in a better fashion than the first time. I can tell you right now that I'll get by. The first time, I didn't know I could, but experience teaches you the pros and cons of life. That's why you left me before, lack of experience. Immature, I believe, was your word for it."

He reached for her, but her eyes blazed sizzling anger that stopped him. He started to speak, checked himself and turned to the door. He stood with his hand on the knob, his back to her for a moment.

"I love you, April. Don't send me away like this."

She didn't answer him, and after a dark moment he went out the door, closing it behind him without looking back.

It was a familiar scene. Finally, everything was familiar. The hurt look on his face, the entreaty for her to understand, the finality of a closing door separating her from the man she loved.

The years drifted past her like slides of a movie projector. They didn't matter anymore. All that mattered was the present—the unbelievable, shattering present.

Chapter Fifteen

She needed to throw something, to commit an act of violence that would release the disbelieving pain in her chest. If she could wrench the sink from the counter and heave it through the window, it would help. In the silent movies the hero would beat on his breast to show his anguish. She needed something more intense, something solid she could smash in her helpless fury.

Six years ago Russ had shattered her completely. She had allowed him to come very close to destroying her. Not Russ; she must be fair. Her love for him had been the destructive agent; he had simply abandoned her.

Marriages end in divorce all the time. What were the last statistics she had read? One out of three marriages end in divorce. One out of three women allowed men to rule their lives enough to change their destiny. For better or worse—that was in the marriage ceremony, not in the divorce papers.

But that was what it meant to women. For better or worse, you are now a divorced woman. Hers had been far worse than she could have imagined. At least for a time. It had taken a year or two, but she managed, after a fashion.

Perhaps we would never have met again except for the accident, except for the amnesia, except for the act of kindness on Russ's part. An old family friend had come to check on her, to see that she was all right. Finding her all right but for the amnesia, he decided he could find out if April was still the immature wife he had divorced many years ago.

"You can't say that I didn't cooperate fully, Russ, just the way I always did where you were concerned. Anything you wanted, I always managed. Except for what I couldn't give you. Experience. Sexual experience." She laughed out loud, and Brush sat up to look at her.

"How about that? You come back to see if my experience has matured me, only to find you're all I've ever had. Serves you right that April remained in limbo as far as sex is concerned for six years. You came back to find exactly what you left behind. I call that poetic justice." She laughed again, the harsh sound hurting her throat.

Crossing the room, she stooped to pick up the papers scattered around the metal box in which she kept her important papers. The divorce papers, stapled to the blue backing to keep them from wrinkling, were lying on the couch where Russ had dropped them.

They were crumpled, and she smoothed them out, replacing them in the folder that had slid beneath the divider and stuck there. Perhaps she had done that on purpose, keeping them out of the way so she wouldn't have to touch them. People do things like that for self-protection, she had read somewhere.

People do a lot of crazy things for self-protection: lie to themselves, develop amnesia to make it easier.

She had waited six years for the amnesia, but it had come at a most opportune time, especially for Russ.

Tucking the papers between the file dividers in the box, she closed it and went to put it back on the top shelf in the closet till the next time she needed it. She stood looking up at the box where it sat on the shelf. A few hours ago, when she reached for it, she had been April Hayden, deeply in love with Russ Calloway. Now she was divorced from Russ—for the second time. Hate for Russ would rid her of the love.

Turning away, she went to open the couch, stiffening a moment before she touched it. She had to sleep somewhere; the couch was all she had. Let it remind her of Russ. That way, she wouldn't likely forget what he had done to her.

Work. Work had always been her salvation. Glancing at her watch and seeing that it was ten o'clock, she dialed the number at the truck stop. Elsa wouldn't be there, but someone could check her schedule.

Wade Outen answered. Wade, who had asked her to go out with him for as long as she could remember. And as long as she could remember, she had refused. She had no reason not to go out with him, especially now.

"It's April, Wade," she said, and didn't bother to tell him she now remembered everything that had ever happened to April Hayden, née Calloway. Née, a legal term for "no longer." "Would you check to see what my schedule is?"

"Ace Movers wants you tomorrow," he said. "And San Bernardino on Monday, but I'll take that one for you."

"Thanks, Wade," she said, "but I'll be able to make it. I'd forgotten I can go after I see Dr. Sarter."

"Sure thing," he said agreeably.

She took Brush out, hoping she wouldn't run into anyone in her robe but not really caring. People who lived around her were just like her; they lived their own lives and let everyone else do the same. That was the way she liked it.

In bed she forced her mind to go ahead to the job tomorrow, not backward into the broiling anger churning through her. She thought she'd lie awake all night, but sleep blanked out the events of the evening, and she didn't wake at all until the radio came on.

She ate breakfast without a chance to talk to Elsa but left her a note on her napkin. "I remember everything, Elsa. Nothing spectacular—I could have saved myself the trouble of worrying about it. Headaches gone for good."

The note would tickle Elsa; they had enjoyed little jokes for years. Elsa need never know this joke was on April.

Before the sun came over the horizon, she was at the loading dock of Ace Movers, a company that had been after her for a long time to do short-haul local transfers for them. She had always been too busy before, but today she didn't have anything to do, and she'd have to be busy to keep her sanity.

How long this time, she wondered. How long will it take me to get over Russ now? Now—after I've found out that I've never really loved anyone but him and that he can still handle my emotions the same as when I was twenty-one?

A shiver of dread shook her as she stared ahead at the traffic.

HE DIDN'T GO HOME but turned the car instead toward Folsom, parking above Folsom Lake not long afterward. It was late, and most of the people had left the recreation area except those in motor homes camped for longer periods.

Since coming home from overseas, Russ had visited the lake several times, needing the quiet solitude of the surroundings, needing to keep his thoughts free of troublesome memories.

Often those memories had been of April, the young April he had left behind him in order to grow. After finding her again, it had been impossible to explain how wrong he had been. She didn't remember him, but there was no denying the spark that flared between them. His making love to her had been inevitable; he hadn't tried hard enough to stay away from her.

She would never believe that he planned to ask her to marry him again. He wouldn't be able to convince her that he had never stopped loving her no matter how many other women he held over the years.

Through the darkness, as he sat there, only lights from campers visible to him, he could see the young April's eyes as he left her: blank, disbelieving. He saw the older April as she looked tonight: disbelieving, hating him for what he had done to her.

This isn't solving anything, he thought, starting the car to drive back toward the city. He let himself into his parents' house in the early hours of the morning, walking quietly to the room he occupied. Was April lying awake thinking of him? Was she crying? She had cried when he left the first time, but it didn't change his mind. It hurt to see her cry, but it didn't convince him to stay.

Remembering the expression on her face tonight was harder. This was a grown-up April, back in love with the man she didn't know had been her husband. Until tonight.

He heard his mother get up and go into the kitchen, giving her time to get the coffee made before he went to join her.

"I make terrible coffee," April told him, and he knew it was true. He had never been able to figure out how someone who could turn out a meal such as she did could absolutely ruin a pot of coffee.

"Why, Russ," his mother said, turning as he entered the kitchen, "what in the world are you doing up so early?"

They never mentioned that he was seeing April again after he asked if they thought seeing them might help April. Their immediate refusal made him wonder a little, but they felt bad about the divorce, no doubt, and didn't want to get caught in the middle.

When he brought her to the house, forcing them to talk to her, telling them they would marry, they accepted it, although he sensed an uneasiness in them. He knew the idea of April's amnesia bothered them and that the idea of his marrying her while she didn't know who she was upset them. It didn't change his mind. If he could have her that way, he'd take his chances on what would happen should she regain her memory.

He had found out.

April's memory was back now, and she didn't need anyone to help her. He sat down at the table, looking at his mother as she poured two cups of coffee.

He had to talk to someone. "April has her memory back, Mother," he said. "She remembered everything last night."

Her swiftly indrawn breath was the only sound she made, and he went on after a moment. "She remembered that I left her, that I never checked to see if she was doing okay after I went overseas. I guess the letter that came back to me wouldn't have made any difference, since it was three years after the divorce."

He picked up the spoon by his cup, glancing at her as he went on. She carefully avoided his eyes. "You and Dad—you didn't try to help her, either, after I was gone, did you? You avoided her so you wouldn't have to make excuses for me; isn't that right?"

She didn't have to nod her head, but she did. He sat there trying to visualize what it must have been like for April to be abandoned by everyone she loved all at the same time.

Cheap and vulgar, she said. You made my love seem cheap and vulgar. Obscene. And for the first time he did see what he had done to her. *Repeated offenses are worse than the first time,* he thought. It would take a long time to erase the past two weeks from April Hayden's mind. But he could try.

He called the home office in ARCOT in San Francisco and talked to the man who had given him the Sydney assignment, requesting a two-week extension of time at home; he got it.

Then he went to camp on April's doorstep.

INSTEAD OF ONE NIGHT in San Bernardino, April stayed until Wednesday. She took in a local rodeo; she walked on the beach, romping with Brush; she sat for hours doing nothing.

Late Tuesday, she called Elsa to tell her she had decided to stay over and to check her schedule for Thursday. She would be coming back to San Bernardino. Good. A longer trip than some; that would help.

"Call Ace Movers for me, please, Elsa. Tell them I'll be available again Saturday if they need me."

Elsa mumbled something about working too many hours but agreed to make the call for her.

It was Saturday night before she parked at Maxwell's again, and instead of going home, she signed for a room. That, in itself, wasn't too unusual; her staying away from home over a weekend was, but Elsa wasn't there, so she didn't have to explain. It didn't matter to her or Brush where they stayed as long as it was clean and comfortable. They were together.

She had become quite successful at keeping her mind blank since Tuesday night. It wasn't as difficult as she imagined it would be. She merely refused to think about Russ. If the aching void became too noticeable, she let herself remember, just for a few minutes, the hours she had spent in his arms. Knowing how he must be congratulating himself on his being able to fool her so completely was enough to erase the thought of him with anger. She refused to let the anger linger, because that made it so much more noticeable. She simply wiped him from her consciousness.

Monday was a month in coming around, she thought as she went through her routine of checking her rig, tires, mirrors, before setting out on her trip.

Rounding the back of her truck, she stopped to wait for Brush to catch up with her. As she turned, she saw the car Russ had been driving parked near the side door of the café.

Without stopping to think about it, she scooped Brush up into her arms, climbed into the truck already idling and pulled from the parking lot. An early-morning confrontation with Mr. Calloway was not on her agenda.

San Bernardino was a lovely city, and while her rig was being unloaded, she found a park nearby. With Brush on a leash looped over her arm, they wandered around, then chose a bench near a clear lake to sit and watch other people as they strolled by.

It was too late to make the return trip that night, but she was on her way north early the next morning. It had now been a week since she discovered how treacherous Russ was. A week was all the time she would give to getting over him—this time. The first time, she was a child; in six years she must have learned something. Give her the two weeks of amnesia to make a fool of herself again and a week to get over it. That was all she needed.

As she parked her rig in an empty slot back of Maxwell's, she didn't bother to look around for Russ's car. He had as much right to eat at the café as she did, and she couldn't possibly avoid him if he chose to do so. She had to work, and Maxwell's was her base of operations.

Checking the schedule, she saw that Ace Movers requested her for the next two days. That would put her up to the weekend. Maybe Ace could use her then, too, if she let them know she was available.

She sat at the counter, ordering a light meal from Katie. "Mom's been wondering what happened to you," the girl said as she placed coffee in front of April.

"Tell your mother I have to make money so I can afford to eat in her establishment."

Katie laughed and went on about the business of serving other customers.

"Where you been, April?"

She turned. "Hi, Wade. Down south."

"I see you finally agreed to haul for Ace Movers. They'll work you to death."

She sent a smile his way. "Good. I need the money."

"Planning to retire soon?"

She nodded. "I'm seriously considering it," she told him, and felt rather than saw him swing around to face her.

"You're kidding."

The toe of her boot hooked behind the stool as she looked at him. "Well, yes, I guess I am kidding. But it would be nice."

"We could go into partnership. Teaming up on the long trips could be fun." His voice was light, but she sensed he could get serious if she allowed it.

I really should go out with him, she thought, her eyes going over the man sitting next to her. *But it would be unfair to Wade. That wouldn't bother some people, but it does me.*

She shook her head, thinking of Russ. A few minutes later she paid her check and went home.

The apartment had the familiar musty smell from being closed, and she opened the window to the night air. Brush sniffed around the familiar spots, drank the fresh water she fixed for him and hopped onto the couch, turning around several times before dropping with a sigh.

She watched him perform the usual ritual, letting her gaze go over the couch she had avoided for over a week. Stubbornly, she allowed her thoughts to return to the evening she last saw Russ, his mouth tight with worry over finding her door locked and not getting any answer from her when he called.

When she threw her accusations at him, he hadn't denied any of it. He couldn't. It was all there, held in his hands, the evidence of what he had done to her years before. And there she stood in front of him, current evidence in his latest accomplishment.

She was ripe, ripe for his conquest. How well she had fit into his scheme of things. He knew her body, knew its response to him. She didn't have a prayer when Russ made up his mind to seduce her.

That's an odd word to use for an ex-husband, she thought. And yet he had seduced her, aided and abetted by his victim. He lit the fires again that once had flamed for him, fires that she didn't know had once burned happily out of control.

It wouldn't take her as long this time. She was older; she knew how to handle out-of-control flames. And where fires once burned, she would douse them; where she had once smothered Russ, she would completely stamp out the flames that now threatened her.

Standing by the sink to drink a glass of water, she looked at the wall calendar. Russ was due to leave for Australia two days ago. She waited for some reaction to show inside her, and when it didn't, she shrugged. When she saw his car at the café, he was probably telling Elsa good-bye and hadn't been looking for her at all. That was, at least, easy to believe.

So he was gone. She no longer had to run from him. Perhaps she never had. Perhaps he had welcomed her dramatic rejection of him and gotten a good laugh from her throwing him out of her small apartment, out of her life. He was ready to move on to bigger and better things.

"I hate to do this, fella," she told Brush, "but I'm tired. Let's get this bed made so I can join you."

The fresh linens looked inviting, and she dropped onto the couch after kicking off her boots and shrugging out of her clothing. She was stretching to relieve her cramped muscles when the knock startled her. Glancing at Brush, she shrugged and went to the closet for her robe. Before she could get it on, there was a more insistent knock, and the doorknob rattled.

"April?"

She stopped in mid-stride at the sound of Russ's voice. Brush barked and ran toward the door where he heard a voice he recognized.

Oh, no, she thought.

She waited. Again came the imperative knock and the demanding voice. "April?"

Drawing in a deep breath, she stood stiffly in the center of the room as she said evenly, "What do you want?"

"I want to talk to you, April. I have to talk to you."

"Say whatever you have to say. I'll listen."

"No. Let me in." His voice was quiet now, pleading with her as he stood outside the door.

Pleading for what, she wondered. Hadn't he taken all she had to give him? Couldn't he be happy with partial destruction? Or did he have to see her crumble all the way before he would be satisfied?

Slowly, she walked across the room. All right, let him see what he's done. She unlocked the door and stood aside as he looked quickly at her, then around the room, before he stepped through the doorway.

Pushing the door closed, she leaned against it, staring at the man who had ruined her—not once, but twice. He looked the same. The lines were etched clearly around his mouth; pain was evident in the light blue of his eyes. She had thought it pain before, associated no doubt with the kidnapping. Maybe she was wrong; he used his eyes to convey meanings to people that were not necessarily so.

His hand came out to her, then dropped to his side. "Whatever I say will sound like a cliché, April, but you have to listen to me."

She didn't answer or move, and she saw him swallow before he went on. "I don't expect you to forgive me right away, but don't condemn me forever." His mouth worked, but no words came out. She stared curiously.

"I didn't know you were all alone when I left to go overseas. My parents told me they'd look after you until you could make it alone. I didn't know that when I left, they decided it would be best not to have any contact with you."

He read the disbelief in her eyes and said again. "I didn't know."

He spoke the truth, she realized. He had gone looking for someone more mature than April, but he hadn't meant to leave her all alone.

"I thought you were leaving for Australia," she said, realizing as she said it that it didn't pertain to their conversation at all.

"I was, but I asked for an extension. I couldn't leave you like this."

"I'm fine," she said, and walked around him to sit on the edge of the couch. "You can leave the country with a clear conscience."

Chapter Sixteen

"Will you listen to me, April?"

"Do I have a choice?" She sat down on the edge of the bed, absently patting Brush as he curled beside her. He, at least, was a solid breathing body, warm and close to her, giving her something she loved to hang on to.

Russ's breathing was loud in the room, and she was conscious of his big hands, opening and closing into fists. He came slowly toward her, and she stiffened, but he moved to the opposite side of the couch and sat down.

"I told you my wife and I divorced because we were too young to make a go of marriage. I was the one who was too young, not you, April. You did what you were supposed to do." He hesitated, then went on. "I was too wrapped up in what I was trying to do and what I thought I was missing to see what I had with you."

She listened to his apology, knowing it hurt deeply to have to tell her this after all the years in between, after a few days of making love to her when she was ignorant of everything else except the fact that she loved him. She loved him as she had when she was twelve, when she was sixteen, when she married him at eighteen.

There had never been anyone for April; no one had ever touched her except Russ, except the man who sat beside her, apologizing for all the heartache he had caused her.

"When the terrorists took Winton and me, you were all I could think about. You stayed with me during the days in the dirty hole they kept us in. I swore if I got out of it alive, I'd find you again."

Her head came up. "You thought I'd still be waiting for you, Russ? You thought I had nothing better to do than to sit back here in California, half a world away from you and your important job, and wait on the chance that you'd remember I was here and come back for me? You knew you were my whole world, so you figured no one would ever come along to take your place?"

He didn't look away from her; the only expression that changed was the familiar tightening of his mouth, the lines that dug deeply into his cheeks.

"No," he denied. "You were the only one I could bet on being the same. You never changed."

"That was my problem, wasn't it? I never changed. I was April, still eighteen when you needed someone thirty. Someone to give you a more satisfactory kind of love, not a child who was nothing if not a one-man, once-in-a-lifetime, wife. I never changed. You're right. From the day I saw you next door, I never changed. Only one way, and that was just to love you more."

Her fingers clenched into Brush's coat, and the small dog raised his head questioningly. She forced her hand to relax. Oddly enough, her thoughts went to his parents. How lost she had been when they cut her out of their lives the same as Russ did. How empty the days had become when she wandered in and out of the weeks and months that followed their separation.

She remembered the final day when she gave up on him and let her sorrow get the best of her, the day she accepted the fact that Russ was gone for good. Russ and his parents said it was up to her to make a go of it alone. And she had.

She stood up and walked to the window, pulling the curtains back to look out on a dark world. Her world had been so dark that no pinpoint of light had beckoned her; no one or no thing had waited for her when she came home to the apartment she had shared with Russ for three years.

The curtain dropped from her hand as she turned back to face him. Once before he had walked away from her. Now he expected her to be ready to go with him anywhere he chose. He'd even marry her again, whether she knew who she was or not. He knew. He knew she still loved him, was there when he wanted her, would always love him. He could bet on it.

"Tell me," she said, her voice very quiet. "Tell me how different it is to make love to April Hayden, six years later."

"April, don't," he said.

"But I need to know, Russ. I need to know if I grew up or if I changed enough to suit you." She moved to stand in front of him, her hands clasped loosely behind her back. "I'm naturally curious. I couldn't satisfy you six years ago; how about now, Russ? I'm sorry I couldn't give you the benefit of a very wide sexual experience, but I guess I never considered it necessary. It just never occurred to me that one day you'd come back to check me out."

He stood up, reaching toward her, but she backed away. Her expression changed from one of pleasant inquiry to a stiff hurt that stopped him.

"Sit down and let me talk to you, April. Let me tell you that I love you. If you want to start over again from the very beginning, that's what we'll do, but I'd like the chance to prove I love you like no one has ever been loved.. I want to make up for all you went through alone. Believe me, I didn't know my parents—"

"Ah, don't blame them, Russ. Didn't they explain it was because they didn't want to interfere, didn't want to have any contact with April Hayden, who no longer belonged to the Calloways? In any way."

She laughed, and his head jerked at the harsh sound. "Make up to me what I went through? Really? It's inside of me, Russ. You can't see the scars, you can't see the deep stabs and bruises, because over the years they've healed. But they're there."

Holding the robe close to her, she went around the edge of the couch and sat back down. Her shoulders slumped but only for a moment, and she straightened to look around at him as he spoke

"I know what you're saying, honey. I know everything you tell me is true. Let me spend the rest of my life making up what I can to you."

The room faded, and she saw herself at twenty-one, remembering exactly the pain that sawed her in half no matter how she struggled to overcome it. She saw the small pickup truck as it hurtled through the air, striking her rig, giving her a respite from her memories for a few weeks. Those memories had grown dim, and she no longer took them out to examine the hurt they left behind. Even the kidnapping had brought only a natural worry to her. Nothing soul wrenching, only a normal uneasiness at the extent of vulnerability the world lived in.

Russ had moved back into her life as easily as he moved out when he saw his chance. April's love was a magnet, pulling them together, giving Russ the solid security of that love when he needed it so badly. It helped him escape from the tortured memories of being held by terrorists and threatened with every horror under the sun.

Standing there, she thought in surprise, *I don't really hate him for that; how could I blame him for a need to rid himself of cold fear if he could find it in my arms? Wouldn't I have expected the same thing from Russ? Wouldn't he have done the same for me?* The only difference was that he'd never come around to see if she needed rescuing from her own demons.

His eyes roamed over her face and came back to meet hers, dark as night in her pale face.

"You don't intend to even try to forgive me, April? You'll let the love we shared die without a chance?" He stood over her, long arms akimbo at his sides in the old stance she could never forget as long as she lived.

"I want to marry you; I want you to go with me to Australia." She didn't answer, and he went on. "I love you, April."

The silence filled the room, their breathing the only sound. She had no idea how long they stayed that way until he reached into his pocket and withdrew a paper, dropping it beside her on the couch.

"I'll cancel my extension, then, if there's no reason for me to stay."

She sat quietly, her eyes on the folded paper near her hand. He turned to walk slowly to the door. "April?"

She shook her head without looking up at him and heard the door open and close, his steps echoing on the stairs as he ran down them, away from her.

In the emptiness of the room, she sat. Her shoulders grew stiff, and she shrugged to rid herself of the tension. She dropped the robe on the floor, reached to turn out the light and heard the rustle of paper as whatever it was he dropped near her fell from the couch.

Beside her, Brush sighed a tired sound that made her smile. She turned on her side. The headache was gone, leaving her limp, with a peculiar sense of euphoria. The emotion-packed hours of the day had taken their toll, and she fell into a drugged sleep.

HER FIRST THOUGHT was that the headache was gone; her second one, that it was Saturday and she had no schedule. She smiled to herself without opening her eyes. Russ would come by, and they would—

Bright pinpoints of pain stiffened her body beneath the light covers. Russ was gone. She had let him go even though he begged forgiveness for what he had done to her.

He didn't have to ask forgiveness. She had forgiven him years ago, but she hadn't forgotten.

Somewhere she had read that if you didn't forget, then you hadn't forgiven. Perhaps not.

I forgot for a few weeks, she remembered. *I forgot long enough for you to do a repeat performance, Russ. And you took advantage of that, didn't you? Oh, yes, you were right there to take all the love I'd saved for you all these years.*

"Oh, God," she moaned softly, turning her face into her pillow.

It would start all over again—the aching, hurting loneliness, the bottomless pit of scathing pain, raking her insides, tearing away the insulation she had carefully built over it during the past years. Russ was a chemical engineer, capable of spraying her soul with acid to destroy her, the acid of contempt he showed by taking advantage of her not knowing who he was, of accepting her love as his due because at one time she belonged to him.

She had tried to tell him she didn't know much, that she had had little experience in the realm of sex. But he had taught her. He had been glad to lead her, to show her how to please him.

And what about him? Yes, Russ knew how to satisfy her, but he always knew that. She hadn't been hard to please; all she wanted from him was love in return for all she had to give.

Throwing back the covers, she stood up, stumbling toward the bathroom to wash her face. It did little to clear her mind, and she went back into the other room, stooping to pick up her robe. A piece of paper lay nearby.

Russ had dropped it on the bed, and she didn't look to see what it was. Now she bent to retrieve it, sitting on the couch to unfold it.

It was a marriage license made out to April Hayden and Russell Calloway, dated the day before. He really intended to marry her. Since her memory returned, she had vaguely wondered if he actually intended to marry her and take her to Australia or whether it had been just his line. He asked for an extension of time, though. At least he said he did.

"I'll cancel my extension," he had told her as he left. It would be easy for him. Russ was footloose and fancy free; he could come and go as he pleased.

With an odd sense of having been down that road before, she moved to the closet to reach for the metal box. Kneeling on the floor, she opened it, dropped the marriage license behind the first divider and replaced the box on the shelf.

As she turned away, she became aware of stinging in her throat, a warm surge of moisture in her eyes, and the room blurred. The damage inside her became a throbbing ache left by the fires of her love for Russ, leaving her scars stripped of protective tissue she had built up over the years. The flaming love had swept over her again with nothing to control it. Fed by her unending love for him, the fires had erupted and spread through her, burning their way with no danger of being stopped.

She cried; cried for the first time in years, and when the dryness choked her, she got up and washed her face, holding her hands, cupped with cool water, to her eyes.

Fervently, she wished for a trip today, a trip anywhere so that she could think about her responsibility for her cargo rather than how well Russ had destroyed her—for the second time. Some of her tears had been for the young couple she remembered, but most of them were for April Hayden of today.

A splotched face stared back at her from the mirror—a red nose, a twisted mouth. Turning away, she went to dress. She fixed the couch, folded the sheets and tucked them away. Brush trotted to the door, and she followed him, picking up her handbag on the way.

Bright sunshine lit the morning, and she squinted. Her eyes were swollen from crying, and she searched in her bag for sunglasses, drawing them out to slip them on.

Through with his survey of the yard, Brush came bouncing back to her, and she walked with him to the car. She had no destination in mind when she got in and pulled away from her parking place.

HE HAD BEEN HOME, but he hadn't slept. For hours he sat in the big chair his dad always used in the living room. He stared at the two photographs of him on the mantel and reminded himself he was going to ask where his wedding pictures were. April and Russ. He wasn't going to be able to marry her again as he thought he would, and he needed something tangible that said she had once belonged to him.

He couldn't let her go. Even knowing she couldn't accept any justification for what he had done, he knew he couldn't let her go.

I'm not the kind to do penance the rest of my life for that mistake, he thought, *so I must convince her she can't live without me, either. I don't know what kind of argument I can use, but there has to be some way to let her know that I love her more than life itself. Other than telling and showing her, which she doesn't believe.*

He leaned forward, elbows on knees. April's body close to his was all he could think about. Her pliant softness as she gave herself to him brought the tenseness to his thighs, the heated muscular contraction throbbing with the memory. He could feel her in his arms, tightly held, responding to his love the way young April had always done. With the torturing difference that it had been a long time for her since he made love to her. He knew without her saying so that no one else had ever touched her that way.

Immature. He had called her immature. Not enough woman for him. She was now. More woman than he had ever met; he didn't want to meet any more. April was the only one for him. Since she was sixteen, he had wanted her.

He heard his mother go into the kitchen, and he got up and left, unable to face her with April's accusations ringing in his ears. Not only had he failed her, but his parents had, too. He willingly assumed blame for both, but right now he couldn't make himself talk to her as though they were all innocent of the wrong they had done to April. There really weren't any excuses for what they had done.

Without thinking, he drove to Maxwell's, looking around automatically for April's rig. It was there, parked just as she had parked it late Friday when she came in. He knew she didn't make many trips over weekends unless it was an emergency or as a favor to one of her customers once in a while. Elsa had told him that.

When she first started, she had worked seven days a week, but as soon as her rig was completely paid for, she had gone to five days a week most of the time. He still found it hard to believe that April, built with a slender frame, handled the big rig as easily as he would be able to do.

He sat in a booth at the back of the café, smiling at Katie as she brought him coffee and took his order. He wasn't hungry, but he could make a pretense of eating as he waited to see if April would come in as she usually did.

"How's it going, Russ?"

Wade Outen stood by the booth, a cup of coffee in his hand, grinning down at him. Russ nodded and motioned to the seat opposite him.

Wade shook his head. "I'm on my way out. Elsa tells me your leave's about up and you'll be going soon."

He nodded. "In a few days."

"I'll be gone a week and a half. If I don't see you..." He held out his hand, and Russ stood up to shake it. He waved his coffee cup and moved away toward the cash register.

The man who possibly was in love with April—what would he say if he knew his relationship to her? He would be astonished, to say the least, to know that April was married to him at one time. As far as anyone at the truck stop was concerned, April had never been married.

She wasn't interested in any man; as far as they could tell, she never dated. She worked, and if she dated, it was someone away from Maxwell's.

Katie brought his breakfast, and he dawdled as much as he could, but April didn't come in. He paid his check finally and left the café. Without thinking, he drove by the building housing her small apartment, remembering he still had the key he had borrowed from the owner. He parked near the office door and went inside.

A young man he had never seen was at the desk. "I came by to borrow a key one day and forgot to return it. Would you see that it's returned to the right place?" He handed it to him and watched as he hung it behind him on a frame before he turned to go out again.

April's car was gone. He stood in the warm sunlight, wondering where she was. He couldn't begin to guess. Was she all right? She said the headaches were gone, but he began to feel uneasy as he remembered the look on her face: the crushed expression, the empty dark eyes. Where would she go if not to Maxwell's?

She had never mentioned friends. When he left her to go with ARCOT, they had only a few acquaintances. Both of them had been busy, working and studying—and loving. They needed few others besides each other and his parents. He recalled a lot of laughter when he and April were married, when she loved to tease him as well as his parents, laughing as she did it.

"A lot of years ago, darling," he murmured aloud. The regret was deep within him, as it had been for years. But the sorrow he felt now was so much more, because he had found her again, only to lose her. If only he had told her it was she who had been his wife; if only he had been able to convince her of his undiminished love for her.

He got back into the car, glancing once more at the window that was at the front of her apartment. That one room she claimed as home—she and Brush.

He'd wanted her to regain her memory, but deep inside he'd hoped they would be married by then and he'd never let her go—no matter what.

There had to be a way to convince April he loved her beyond everything else.

Chapter Seventeen

The direction in which she drove was aimless; she wasn't going anywhere in particular. Without thinking about it, she headed west, away from her usual routes. The car she drove was old, and now she remembered why she kept it. The Calloways had given them the down payment as a wedding present. They had just paid it off and received the title when Russ left her.

Smiling a little, her eyes following the white ribbon down the center of the road, she remembered their celebration when the title came in the mail. They had bought a bottle of the cheapest California wine from Napa Valley that they could find.

Russ could afford champagne and the most expensive of the wines now. ARCOT furnished him with a car, so he didn't have to be burdened with that expense. Most of the mileage she covered was in the rig, and a nine-year-old car served her purpose as well as any.

Somewhere along the highway she stopped to have coffee and an English muffin, let Brush out to romp and got back into the car. At Vallejo, she turned south through Concord, Antioch, Stockton, ending up at

Manteca. From there she turned back north toward Sacramento. It was dark when she pulled into Maxwell's.

Inside, she checked her schedule—back to San Bernardino.

She nodded to acquaintances and sat at the counter, giving Katie her order. "Empty beds tonight, Katie?" she asked.

"Sure, for you, April, always. If Mom had to make me sleep in the kitchen, she'd give you a bunk."

She grinned at the young girl and ate, surprised to find she was actually hungry. *I may yet get back to normal,* she decided, and the realization of what happened sent a chill along her shoulders, raising the hair along the nape of her neck.

Fork poised over the food on her plate, she thought, *I'm far from out of the woods. Time. I need time.*

She went to bed in the small neat room with bunk beds. Originally designed for all male truckers, she seldom shared a room. There weren't that many female drivers in the area. She lay in bed, listening to the sounds of others as they came and went, some just for showers after a long haul; some, like her, staying all night. Sleep didn't come at all, and she was still staring at the ceiling when daylight came through the windows.

Dragging a leaden body, she dressed and went for coffee. Elsa was there, calling orders, moving quickly with the life-sustaining liquid necessary to truckers.

"How are you, April?" she called from the end of the counter.

"Back to normal, whatever that is. Guess I'll go see Dr. Sarter Monday and see what happened to me."

"Anything worth mentioning that you remember?" Elsa asked, pouring more coffee into her cup.

"Sorry. All I recall is Maxwell's and Brush." She laughed a shaky laugh, but Elsa didn't notice. The older woman moved away, and she got up to pay her check.

Outside, she looked around at the parking lot—familiar rigs, all of them. No matter if it did shatter her, getting back her memory was worth it, putting a bit of solid ground beneath her feet. She went home.

MOST OF THE DAY was spent sorting laundry, straightening the small room into severe neatness and avoiding the closet that held the metal box. She cleaned the cabinets over the sink, under the sink and in the bathroom. She dusted and ran the sweeper. All of that kept her busy for two hours, and she was again at loose ends, refusing to think about Russ.

Brush accompanied her to the laundromat, lying in his usual place in the back window of her car as she moved in and out with her clothes. By two in the afternoon, her body began to tell her that she hadn't slept the night before, and as soon as her clothes were folded and put away, she made up the couch and went to bed.

Her outstretched arms could feel the print of Russ's body on the mattress near her, and she pulled them back to her sides. Everything that had happened between them came back, and she swallowed over familiar nausea. Things like this only happened in soap operas and grade B movies. The heroine is rescued in the movies and lives happily ever afterward with the tall, dark and handsome hero.

I'm the soap opera, she thought. The pain is complicated by another tragic happening when John loves Mary instead of Betty, who loves Jack, who is married to Lucy. The ache inside her grew to fill her body; it filled the void Russ left there when he destroyed her love.

The shrill ringing of the phone caused her to jump and Brush to give a short, surprised bark. She rolled over to reach for it, hesitating a moment before picking it up.

Closing her eyes, she said, "Hello."

"April, it's Wade." She let her breath go slowly. Why had she supposed that Russ would bother to call? "Are you sure you feel like taking the San Bernardino run tomorrow?"

"Yes, I'll be able to go, Wade. Thanks."

"Anytime," he said.

Lying back against the pillows, she waited for her heart to stop its hurried beating. Russ wasn't going to call; she might as well accept that. She sent him away, and Russ had his pride; he wouldn't be back. By the weekend he'd be on his way to Australia.

When she woke, it was four-thirty in the morning. She stared hazily at her clock radio, confirming she had slept about twelve hours.

Monday, I have a schedule. First, Dr. Sarter. She rubbed over the left eye, thankful the pain was gone. At least the physical pain. She dragged herself out of bed, hoping a shower would revive her.

Automatically, checking off her list of things to do before leaving for a couple of days, she looked around one last time.

"Let's go, Brush," she said, and closed the door behind her. It wasn't yet daylight as she pulled into

Maxwell's parking lot. The medical center didn't open till nine o'clock. That was going to be an awful lot of coffee to drink between now and then.

Although she took a lot of time with her breakfast, it was still early as she stood up to pay her check, eyes surveying the diners. She answered greetings, waved to others and went stiff with shock as her gaze encountered Russ's light blue eyes.

He was sitting in a booth near the door, and there was no way she could keep from going at least that close to him. He nodded at her and turned back to his coffee.

Somehow she paid her check and walked out the door, keeping her eyes straight in front of her. She was shaking as she got outside. The hurt washed over her again as though it had never subsided, as though just waiting to start its ruinous journey through her body. Fresh pain jerked her body stiffly upright, and she stood there in disbelief as she fought against giving in to the desire to scream at the unfairness of it.

She had given all those years to forgetting Russ, and he was back with a few times of loving her to shatter her world again. Head down, she walked to her rig, going over the routine checkpoints necessary before any trip: tires, mirrors, tools. And through it all she saw Russ, felt his hands on her, his mouth teaching her lips how to respond to him, teaching her body what it was meant to know, what she had really never forgotten over the years.

Russ was glad to give her a refresher course. He had lots of experience from mature women now, experience he could pass on to April, who had none.

It was still early, but she got into her car and drove toward the medical center, taking a paperback novel with her into the waiting room. On a first-come, first-serve basis, she would be the first one to see the doctor.

With the book open in front of her, she sat looking at the printed page. She saw the words—a, an, the, they, them—and all the combinations that made them into a story, but she didn't get any complete thoughts from the page. She gave up trying and sat there, waiting.

Several times the door opened, and people came in, signing the sheet at the desk. Idly, she glanced up as someone came in but didn't go immediately to sign in.

She froze. Russ stood just inside the door, looking at her. There was a questioning tenderness in the light blue eyes, reflecting shadows from the drawn drapes. He crossed the room and took the chair next to her.

"How long will you have to wait?" he asked, as though it were the natural thing for him to be talking to her.

Natural animosity toward the man she loved—or had loved—came to her rescue. Her voice just as level as his, she told him, "I'll be the first one he sees when he starts." She glanced at her watch. "It's another fifteen minutes before his office hours begin."

They sat side by side, not speaking, but she could feel his gaze going over her averted face and sense the animal magnetism between them.

"April?" His whispered question came as the door to the doctor's office opened and the nurse called her name.

Thankfully, she stood up, but he caught her hand. "I'm going to wait. I want to know what the doctor says about you." At her dark look he said, "I'm your husband, April. I have a right to know."

Her whispered answer was fierce. "You aren't my husband. You deserted—"

His hand tightened around her fingers. "Maybe we aren't married yet, but you belong to me."

Yanking her hand away, she turned and walked quickly away from him. That was the wrong thing to say to her. She definitely did *not* belong to him. Her teeth were ground together as she faced Dr. Sarter.

The doctor smiled. "Well, April, how's the headaches?"

"Gone." She told him briefly about the disappearance of the pain, the return of her memory.

He went over her. He flashed several different-sized lights into her eyes, going over her again and again, pressing the area that the week before had been so painful to her.

"I don't want to take any more X rays, April. It hasn't been long enough since the last ones. Tell you what. Next Monday, come in again and let me take a look. Your eyes are clear, there's no evidence of fluid or swelling. That's the best indication of normalcy." He took the instrument he had been using from around his head, looking at her. "If you have even the slightest recurrence of pain, come in right away. I'll call Dr. Wall and send him a copy of my evaluation."

Thanking him, she made her way back to the desk. "I have the insurance papers filled out. Can you get them signed and sent in for me?"

"Of course, Miss Hayden," she was told. "I'll bill you for the balance if there is any."

Russ was standing behind her as she turned. "Everything okay?"

"Yes."

Together, they walked outside. "Will you come with me, April?" he asked.

"No." The one word came from a dry throat, grating harshly through her chest.

He bent and kissed her cheek, then turned and walked away from her. She watched him get into his parents' car and pull out into the street before she climbed into her car and drove back to the truck stop.

It was only a little after ten o'clock when she turned her rig in the direction of San Bernardino. Dr. Sarter was satisfied she was doing fine; the insurance papers were properly filed; Russ was on his way to Australia without her.

His explanation that she belonged to him whether or not they were married made little difference. For some reason she was glad he was there. A traitor he might be, but he cared enough to check on her one final time before he left the country.

The miles rolled beneath her, and the pain receded into a dull ache, one she supposed would be there for some time.

"Happiness is so fragile, Brush, so transient. Here today, gone tomorrow." She expressed her thoughts aloud to her sleeping companion. "I was happy when I was married to Russ, but he wasn't.. I could have been happy again, but would he?" Doubts and uncertainty from the years after her divorce flitted through her mind.

Hers was one of several rigs waiting to be unloaded at the docking platform in San Bernardino, and it would be morning before she was unloaded. She signed for a room and went to bed.

While her truck was being unloaded the next morning, she lingered over breakfast, discussing current events with the trucker sitting next to her.

"I was glad to see they caught the terrorists who kidnapped those guys from ARCOT a few months ago," he said.

Her head swiveled toward him. "I didn't hear that."

He nodded. "Egyptian undercover agents got them. Killed a couple of them and captured several—and recovered most of the ransom that was paid."

In the discovery of her love for Russ, she had forgotten that he had been the victim of that seemingly long ago kidnapping.

What was it he told her? "The thought of coming back to find you kept me going those days in that hole." Something to that effect. She hadn't listened to him. So caught up in her own misery over his deceit, hurting so badly over remembered wounds from when they were so much younger, she didn't think about what Russ had gone through. She refused to listen to his plea that he had been too young, too, those many years ago, refused to hear him when he begged her forgiveness, wanting her love again.

He was gone. There would be no second chance for her, just as she had ignored Russ's entreaty for another chance with her.

Late in starting back north, her nagging thoughts kept her company as she wrestled with the heavy evening traffic on the interstate. It seemed they had moved Sacramento at least a hundred miles farther by the time she pulled in to Maxwell's.

Her schedule listed a trip to Lake Tahoe Wednesday, then back to Susanville on Thursday. She signed her initials to show she had seen it and went home.

Late spring was turning the city to green and sprinkling it with colors as the flowers blossomed in well-tended yards. A rambling rosebush with thick yellow buds grew alongside the steps to her apartment, and she touched them lightly with her fingertips as she passed them. Drawing an appreciative breath of their perfume, she waited for Brush to catch up with her, smiling as he bounded up the steps beside her.

"April?"

Her breath caught as her head came up sharply at the sound of her name, and she looked at the couple who stood outside her door. Mr. and Mrs. Calloway were there.

Swallowing over her shock, she nodded. "Good evening."

"We want to talk to you, April," Mr. Calloway said. He glanced nervously at his wife and went on. "Could we come inside?"

Unlocking the door, she stood aside to allow them to enter, seeing the room as they must see it. Simply furnished, almost bare, but neat and clean. She crossed the room to open the window, turning back to motion them to sit on the couch. Brush nosed curiously around their feet, then jumped on the couch between them to lie down. It was his territory, after all. She didn't tell him to move.

Pulling the small hassock forward, she sat facing them. Mr. Calloway leaned forward, licking his lips. "April."

Mrs. Calloway hadn't spoken, but now she interrupted her husband. "We came to tell you we're sorry." She stopped, realizing how inane the statement sounded. She started over.

"Russ left Monday night, but he told us what happened before he left." Her hands rubbed each other in her lap. "He said it was all his fault, but that isn't true, and you know it as well as we do. We were wrong, April, when we pretended you didn't exist after you and Russ separated. We were hurt to lose you, but we really thought it would be better if we stayed out of it. All the way out of it."

"We didn't know about your illness, April. We drove by several times and saw the car, so we thought you were here and all right since the car was always parked in the same place." Mr. Calloway shook his head. "If we had only stopped, just once, to see about you, but we thought—"

She sat still. The lost and terrified hurt of years ago seemed far away. Perhaps she should have gone to the Calloways and asked for help, but that was in the past. She looked up as Mr. Calloway took up where his wife hesitated.

"After so many years passed and Russ was home a couple of times, we thought you must have remarried. Russ couldn't find you, and he saw a child where you once lived, so he thought you were married and still stayed there."

"I lived in the apartment almost a year after—after Russ left; then I moved to Sacramento," she murmured in the silence.

He nodded. "I guess you had an unlisted phone?"

"I didn't have one for a long time. I got all my messages from the truck stop."

"Oh, April." Mrs. Calloway's eyes filled with tears. "We missed you so much. Would you—could you?" She stopped.

Chin resting in her cupped hands, elbows on her knees, April stared at the two people in front of her. They, along with Russ, had been the only family she had after her parents' death. They had filled the void in the still-teenaged April, and she loved them without reservations. They had failed her, true, but in doing so, they had failed themselves.

Her heart ached for the four of them, for the years of loneliness and unhappiness in all of them, for the love she had been denied, that had deserted her.

If you don't forget, you don't forgive, the old saying went. Maybe the old saying was wrong. They shouldn't ever forget what had happened in order that it should never happen again.

Her shoulders straightened slowly, and she slid forward until she knelt in between the two people sitting there. Brush immediately kissed her cheek, thinking the attention was for him. Simultaneously, the three of them reached for each other and sat quietly that way for a long time.

It was an emotional reunion on both sides. April knew today wouldn't be the end of her resentment. There would be times she would certainly condemn them for the past, but she was going to try. It was too soon after the hurt to shrug her shoulders and let bygones be bygones. She would have liked for it to be that way, but she, too, was human, and it would take her some time to be as she was years ago.

Perhaps she'd never be the same—and who was to say that was all bad? People should change, not in love but in their concept of what love should be.

In the days that followed, she made her scheduled runs, calling the Calloways when she was in town. It was almost two weeks before they heard from Russ, a short cable that said he had arrived in Sydney and was being sent immediately to the ARCOT station isolated in the Snowy Mountains.

April held the impersonal piece of paper in her hand, reading the brief message again.

"Arrived safely. Duty in Snowy Mountains. Return about two weeks. Will write."

She had eaten dinner with the Calloways, a menu far more involved than what she usually had on any Sunday when she snacked or went to Elsa's.

"I have his address if you want to write him, April," Mrs. Calloway said.

She nodded and at home that night started a letter to Russ. After a few minutes, she gave up.

How do you tell a man you love him when, after all, you've let him know he's quite low in your estimation? You've told him you never want to see him again; you've let him see the bitterness in you without any indication you might relent.

Just tell him, her inner self urged. *Write and tell him.*

But she didn't. She postponed writing until she returned from Susanville, then again, until after her San Diego trip. That didn't keep her from thinking about him with every turn of her wheels. Every night she dreamed about him, holding him close at least while she slept and awakening to an emptiness stretching days and weeks ahead of her.

Russ had been gone over a month, and there had been only the one short cable from him. Sometimes she wondered at the reality of it all, but she heard his voice telling her he loved her, felt his arms around her, saw the entreaty in his eyes as he begged her to forgive him.

Four days straight on the road left her totally ex-hausted, and she couldn't wait to get out of her rig so her body could relax. Collecting her mail from Elsa, she tucked it into the side pocket of her handbag and headed for home.

Chapter Eighteen

The flight to Australia was long and tiring. He changed planes in Honolulu with a two-hour wait before resuming the flight. He sat in the cocktail lounge with an exotic drink in front of him, thinking of the day he and April shared a Lovers' Volcano, then went to the tiny apartment she lived in and made love.

That was the day he noticed how tired she looked, dark circles beneath her eyes and a restless habit of rubbing over the scar left when she hit the steering wheel of her truck. He saw again the puzzled look on her face when he said they had to get married.

Smiling, he heard her say. "We don't have to get married; I'm not pregnant."

He knew she wasn't, too, and had been careful in that respect. Whatever else she accused him of, he had protected her in that. Loving her so much, wanting her to remember him but dreading it, he had taken her because he couldn't help himself. Again and again, she belonged to him, and he wanted their marriage more and more after each possession of the slim body that had belonged to him so many years ago.

April was still an innocent sexually. All she knew about giving herself to a man he had taught her. But when she turned to him to be loved, she knew how to give herself to him, how to take his love for her.

Dear God, he thought, despair in his chest as he stared into the afternoon sunlight of the tropical island. *She'll never forgive me, nor will I blame her. But how am I going to live without her again?*

The flight continuing on to Sydney was called, and he made his way to the gate, paying no attention to the singing and dancing going on around him, to the welcoming committee of Polynesian beauties native to Hawaii, smiling, giving kisses and leis of baby vanda orchids.

The first-class seat in the plane was comfortable, and as the big jet leveled off at cruising altitude, he adjusted the seat back and closed his eyes. April's vision settled itself on his lids, her mouth twisted with the pain of what she had just discovered—her divorce papers from Russell Calloway.

He drifted into sleep, thankful to lose the memory of April's accusations for a little time.

It was early morning, Sydney time, when the plane landed, and he looked around at the winter scenery. No snow here, but the wind whistled at an uncomfortable pace around the buildings. Late spring in California was a vast distance from the winters of Australia. Not bad, but the ARCOT experiment station was located along the edge of the outback country on the edge of the Snowy Mountains where it was much colder.

He didn't mind the change in weather so much; he had brought the right clothing for it, and as long as you dressed right, you were okay. There would be plenty to occupy his mind out there, and right now that was what he needed, something to keep him from going crazy thinking about April.

He was right. The days passed in a blur of concentrated tests and programs as he learned what was different about the ARCOT business in Australia compared to the one in Egypt. His six years in that country, traveling to any number of other nations during that time, had trained him well in the business climate of the company.

Russ Calloway was now one of their top chemical engineers, brought up through the ranks from the probationary period to top-level management in those years. At thirty-one years old, he was the youngest engineer in the laboratory in Sydney. It didn't bother him to learn that. He knew his job; he was capable.

Studying the ground rules for experiments for the company in the project now in the works, he was up many nights, reading the manuals, studying the formulae. It didn't matter whether he went to bed or not; he seldom slept more than a couple of hours at a time. April woke him often, her haunting smile tearing him apart. He saw the quiet desperation in her as she questioned him, as she told him what happened after he left her.

I wouldn't have left her alone. I know I wouldn't have, he kept telling himself. *If I had known Mom and Dad—* He broke off his thoughts, unwilling to blame his parents for what he himself had done. They had given April up, too, after loving her all those years.

Wearily, he went about looking for an apartment. Webb Lewis, one of the engineers who had been in Sydney many years, gave him an address, and he pulled out the slip of paper to check it against the map he carried. Paddington. Along with his four-wheel-drive jeep, Webb gave him the address of a division of restored town houses he said were available—for a price. As long as the company paid him his fabulous salary, including a housing allowance, he intended to be comfortable. He did a lot of work at home for the company, and good living quarters were a necessity as far as he was concerned.

In amazement he went through what once had been Sydney's inner-city slum area. It now consisted of a tightly packed mass of terrace houses built during the Victorian era. Up and down the steeply sloping streets, it was a fascinating jumble of beautifully restored terraces.

He approached the address written on the card, lifting the heavy brass knocker and letting it fall as he looked around. Shops strongly resembling high-class flea markets and restaurants boasting quaint titles and facades dotted the streets with no abrasion whatsoever into the urban scene.

"May I help you?"

He turned at the broadly accented voice to face a woman smiling at him. "Russell Calloway. Mr. Lewis of ARCOT, International called earlier in the week about a rental you have."

"Of course. Come in, Mr. Calloway."

Thirty minutes later, he had signed the contract for the terrace house she showed him through. Two bedrooms, living room, separate kitchen and huge bathroom, furnished in the traditionally comfortable furniture the Australians were known for. Shades of deep aqua with lighter drifted designs covered the couch cushions. Wall-to-wall carpet of a deep cobalt blue went throughout all the rooms with the exception of the kitchen.

Loosening the tie he had worn for some unknown reason, he pulled it away from his shirt collar, unbuttoning the shirt down three buttons. He looked around at the comfortable plushness and wished for April.

What would she be doing about now? He glanced at his watch, frowning as he tried to remember the time difference. Ten hours, maybe, plus ten hours. If she wasn't on an overnight run, she should be at home. He looked around. There was a place for a phone, but the instrument hadn't yet been given to him to plug in. He went in search of Mrs. Hughan.

THE WASHED-OUT, tired feeling hung on to April as she kept up a tough schedule of runs, keeping busy, trying not to think of Russ. Now, as she lay there, waiting for sleep to overtake her, he was back. Blue eyes met hers with an entreaty she saw day after day. What was he doing? Was he working hard? Did he still have the nightmares about the terrorists?

She shuddered. He was a long way from the terrorist threat in Egypt, but no one was really safe from fanatics, it seemed, no matter where one was.

Her mind grew fuzzy with sleep, and she drifted into the twilight zone of being neither asleep nor awake, waiting for total unconsciousness.

A telephone ringing late at night always has a scary sound, and she sat straight up in bed, staring toward the instrument on the table close by. Her hand was shaking as she reached for it, turning the light switch as she did so.

At first, she didn't hear any voices but a sort of rushing sound as though the call were long distance. She couldn't think of anyone she knew who lived farther away than the Calloways at Brookeville.

"April?"

She pressed the receiver to her ear, sticking her finger in her left one to shut out any other sound. "This is April," she said, speaking loudly.

More static; then suddenly the line cleared, and she heard Russ say, "Can you hear me, April?"

"Russ?" She held up the instrument to look at it, then put it back to her ear. "Russ?"

"Yes. I just got back into Sydney this morning. How are you?"

"I'm fine." Did he call me up from ten thousand miles away to ask about my health, she wondered, her eyes fastened on the frayed edge of the lampshade.

"April, I want you to know that I love you, that every word I said while I was with you is true. I don't know if you can ever forgive us or not, darling, but I'd like you to try."

She made a sound, and he went on. "Don't hang up on me, honey, please. Hear me out." He waited, and when she still didn't say anything, he spoke again. "After you've gotten over some of the hurt, after you've forgiven me a little, would you come out to see me?"

"To Australia?" she asked, trying to picture a trip that far away from California.

"To Sydney. I just leased a terrace house in a very nice section of town, right downtown as a matter of fact."

"What's a terrace house?" she asked, trying to quiet her thudding heart, which had gone on a rampage as soon as it heard his voice.

Deep laughter came over the telephone cable. "I guess it's a combination of town house, condominium and garden apartment, if I was back there. Restored Victorian-era houses on the hills and slopes that make up a lot of the inner city.''

The sound of his laugh sent shivers zipping along her spine, and she smiled in spite of herself. Russ had the nicest laugh, and when he was finished making love to her, his laugh always sounded sleepy, or relaxed—or both. She missed him so much at that moment, she would have walked to Sydney had she been able.

''April?'' She heard his deeply indrawn breath. ''Will you come out?''

''I—I don't know. I—I'd have to see if someone—''

''You'll come? You'll think about it, April?'' He sighed, the feeling making its way across the oceans to caress her body as though he had touched her.

''When can you come, darling? Soon?'' The question lifted her up, prodding her into believing he was begging her to join him.

''Russ?'' Swallowing hard, she waited.

His voice grew quiet. ''Do you forgive me, April? Will you be able to forgive me, do you think?''

She was sure. Her arms were empty; her body longed for the bulwark of his strength, for the satisfaction of loving him. If she couldn't live without him, she could surely forgive him.

''Have you called your parents, Russ?''

It was his turn to hesitate. ''No, April. I had to call you and see if you were all right.''

''Listen, darling,'' she said. And she told him about the Calloways' visit, their long talk about everything that had happened, the reconciliation she hadn't been able to write about.

"I was so unhappy when you left, Russ. I thought I couldn't forgive you; I thought it would lower my opinion of myself if I gave in too easily."

"Oh, darling" was all he said, but it was enough.

"I love you. I want to be with you," she said.

"Listen, sweetheart, I'll check the airline schedules and send you a ticket. When do you think you'll be able to leave? I'll call you when you think you've had time to make the arrangements."

She was trying to think. "How long do you think I should stay?"

"Forever, April. Forever, darling, please." His voice was pleading, and she could see the eyes squeezed shut, with only a line of eyelashes showing between tightly closed lids.

"Oh," she said. "What—what about my rig?"

"You can sell it," he told her. "It's in good shape; you shouldn't have any trouble. Dad will help you."

That's called burning your bridges behind you, she thought hazily, rubbing her forehead. With eyes closed, she thought of Russ, his arms around her, his lips murmuring sweet words and promises. This time she would take care of him in the way a man needed to be taken care of. He would have no reason to seek someone else for his satisfaction. With his coaching, she could learn all she needed to keep him happy. And he could keep her happy, too. With his tutelage, she had found desires within her body she never knew she possessed. A faint flush washed over her, turning her cheeks pink as it reached her face.

"I—I don't know how long it will take me, but I'll try to hurry. Oh, Russ, do you think—?"

"No, I don't think, darling; I know. I'm sure. Are you sure, April?"

"Yes," she breathed into the phone. "Yes, for the first time, I'm sure you love me as much as I love you. That's a lot, Russ."

The quiet laughter came over the miles to turn her knees to water, to start a slow tumultuous throb in her thighs. "You're right; it's enough for at least two life-times, isn't it?"

"Yes."

"April, would you call Mom and Dad and tell them about us? They'll be happy."

"Yes, I will."

His "I love you" and "Good night" ringing in her ears, she sat there after the connection was broken, letting her thoughts go, letting the doubts and confu-sion flit through her consciousness, letting the posi-tive love inside her take over and tell her it was the right thing to do.

She dialed the Calloway number.

Chapter Nineteen

It was a month before she could manage to get everything settled enough to leave California. The truck rig sold immediately; Wade Outen bought it. When it was first advertised, he eyed her with incredulous disbelief.

"You're moving to Australia? April, you can't—" Dull color flushed in his cheeks as she stood looking at him, and he swallowed. Then he shrugged. "It's better for my peace of mind, of course."

All her friends now knew she was marrying Russ. No one knew it would be for the second time.

She watched him with a bit of sadness inside, but she was so happy since the decision to go to Russ that she couldn't stay that way for more than a minute. When he bid on the rig, she gave him a good price, and the deal was closed. Wade would take care of it the same as she had.

The Calloways agreed to let her leave the old car with them. As old as it was, it had only 70,000 miles on it and was still in good condition.

Russ was impatient. Almost every day there was a card or letter from him telling her to hurry. He missed her and loved her. He was becoming used to wintertime over there and warned her to bring warm clothing.

"It doesn't get severely cold as some of our states do, April, but compared to California, it's rather chilly. Bring enough warm clothing to last at least three months. Or you can buy plenty of the proper weight here. Sydney is a big city. I think you'll like the area where our house is located because of the shops and restaurants."

"Our house." It had a nice sound.

In one letter he gave her the regulations regarding pets. "I'm afraid the best we can hope for with Brush is a thirty-day quarantine; sometimes they require ninety days. Make sure all his shots are up-to-date and bring the papers with you, not just the tags."

She was at the Calloways', reading her letter to them. Brush had wandered over to Mr. Calloway and lay near him, his square nose resting on a shoe. The man's work-worn hand dropped to rub Brush, and the little dog sighed, closing dark button eyes in contentment.

"You can leave Brush with us," Mrs. Calloway told her. "Maybe that would be better."

April looked at the little dog, her lone companion for more than four years, and shook her head. "Thanks, anyway, but I'd rather take him. He'll be unhappy in quarantine, but he loves Russ, and I'd be lonely without him." Russ would be away from her at times, she knew, but even if that weren't true, Brush belonged to her and vice versa. She couldn't leave him.

When Russ told her to bring enough warm clothing for three months, she laughed to herself. He hadn't looked in her closet lately. And it was almost summer in California. Warm clothing hadn't been on the racks since Christmas. She would have to stick with the few sweaters and pants she had and buy when she got there.

Methodically, she went through her papers, checking off everything Russ had listed for her to do. In the metal box, she put all of the papers showing Brush had the necessary shots and her health insurance, which she wasn't sure was effective in Australia. Stuck down against the side was a single folded paper she pulled out to look at.

It was the marriage license Russ had purchased the day her memory came back. She sat looking at the paper, marveling at the emotions that paper roused in her. The terrible days and black nights after he left her were but a shadowy recollection now as was the hollow distrust of his vow that he loved her and would make up for all the hurt he had caused her.

Perhaps. Her finger traced the names typed on the license. Perhaps he could erase the bad memories, but if he didn't, there would be more poignant everyday happenings to push the hurting ones away. She had grown up; hurting was a part of growing up.

Even with Russ complaining about the length of time, she sometimes panicked when she tried to think of everything she had to do and the length of time left to get it done. Finally, tickets and reservations in hand, times verified and luggage ready, she placed her call to Russ.

"Tomorrow morning at eight-thirty, Russ," she told him. "My flight is due in Sydney at eight in the evening, your time."

She could hear him breathing, but he didn't say anything. "Russ? You still want me to come, don't you?"

"More than anything in the world, darling. I was just trying to adjust to the fact that you're actually on your way to me. I'll be there to meet you." She smiled as he added, "And April, I love you very much."

Elsa cried; Wade watched her with a smile on his face; dozens of others she had become acquainted with over the years wished her luck.

"I'm coming to visit you as soon as I graduate from school, April," Katie told her. "I've always wanted to go to Australia."

The Calloways had been the same warm family she had before, and they hated to see her leave. "Russ needs you more than we do, I guess," Mr. Calloway told her. "Perhaps we can visit one of these days."

She hugged them. "Of course." She had no idea of the length of company tours in foreign countries, but Russ was always allowed home leave if he wanted it. When she joined him in Sydney, that would be home, he told her when they talked the night before.

She shivered in anticipation as she lay in one of the Calloways' spare bedrooms, Brush close beside her. Too excited to sleep, she closed her eyes and thought of Russ, anxious to have him hold her again. It had been so long.

IT WAS RAINING when the big plane circled Sydney for a landing. Russ had told her that wintertime wasn't the rainy season, but that didn't seem to matter to the sheets of water she saw blowing across the airport.

The navy flannel pantsuit she wore had been found by a saleslady at one of the bigger department stores who recalled packing away some heavier clothing recently during inventory. The pale pink silk blouse reflected a light tint in her cheeks and set off the darkness of her eyes.

Across her arm she carried a navy all-weather coat the Calloways had given her. Apparently it was going to be very handy.

Along with the two hundred or so other passengers, she went up the covered entrance to the waiting area, her eyes busily scanning the crowd.

Where was Russ? For a moment she was frightened. Suppose he had to go somewhere, or the company called him away? She swallowed over the dryness in her throat, and at that moment she saw him. Sandy brown hair, streaked with gray, had been smoothed back but still managed to loosen itself into heavy waves. He was anxiously looking the crowd over when his light blue eyes locked with her dark ones.

The tight lines around his mouth suddenly disappeared as he smiled at her. He didn't try to reach her in the crush of the people moving ahead of her but waited by the roped area until she came even with him. Then he simply reached across and picked her up, hand luggage and all, and lifted her across the ropes into his arms.

His mouth, buried in the thickness of her hair, murmured her name, and he held her close. She gave a tired sigh and leaned against him.

"It's good to be home," she whispered.

Outside the throng of people, they stood holding each other, until he raised his head to look down at her. His eyes were moist as he gazed at her, feature by feature, then bent to place his mouth gently on hers. She wasn't sure whose body trembled—perhaps it was both of them—but he lifted his head to stare at her once more.

He wasn't smiling. There were questions in his eyes even as she recognized the quiet happiness in them.

"April?"

She nodded in answer to his question, realizing he wanted to know if he was forgiven. She had come to him, but had she really forgiven him? Her nod this time was more emphatic, and he pulled her to him once more, holding her to his chest. His heart pounded in her ear, a sound that caressed the vibrant nerves that seemed to be exposed in her body.

He hardly took his hands away from her as he retrieved her baggage. His eyes rested on her face, on her mouth, drinking in her expression as they waited to go through customs. They said little as they passed through the lines and made their way outside to his car.

"What about Brush?" she asked, turning to look at him as he opened the car door.

"He'll be moved to the quarantine area, and we can pick him up in thirty days. I have the ticket for him." He smiled at her. "He'll be all right."

He guided the car out of the airport, and she watched in amazement as he went to the left side of the road and stayed there. He grinned at the questions in her eyes.

"It's the correct way to drive over here, honey. It just takes some getting used to, but be sure you drive on the left side of the road."

"I think I'll do a lot of walking," she said as she watched the curious appearance of all the cars they met being on her side of the car. The rain had let up. Only a thick drizzle fell, and a bluish mist hugged the ground.

He had been holding her left hand on his thigh, and now he squeezed it. "Tired?" he asked as she turned to look at him.

"Sort of light-headed, but I guess that's to be expected."

"Did you sleep on the plane?"

"No. Nor the last two nights, either." At his quick look she smiled. "I'm not sick, just excited."

He nodded, his fingers curling around her hand, sliding it up and down his hard thigh.

"We live over there," he said, pointing to his left. "See the street winding up the hill? That's the area they call Paddy. Used to be a slum, but whoever had the idea to revitalize it came up with a great idea. It's beautiful." He glanced at her. "I hope you'll like it."

"I will."

He smiled a little. "How can you be sure before you see it?"

"I'll be living with you, won't I?"

"You'll be *married* to me, April. There's a difference." He laughed, remembering her question. "No, we don't have to get married, but we are."

She felt a quiet drumbeat in her temple, giving a sort of technicolor to her thoughts. It had been a long time since Russ had held her. The exhaustion beginning to creep over her was creating a sort of haze over everything, and she was glad when he parked alongside the curb in front of a row of terrace houses. His description of a terrace house had been a good one: part town house, part condominium and part garden type, had they been anywhere in California.

Inside, she looked around at the clean, airy spaciousness. Quite a difference from her tiny efficiency that had been home to her for as long as she remembered, or cared to remember.

"Honey?" Russ turned her to face him, his hands moving upward over her arms, across her shoulders, cupping beneath her ears. Long fingers slid into her hair, over her neck, tilting her head back.

His mouth on hers was cool and moved in questioning search across her soft lips. Her breath caught as the tip of his tongue probed gently inside, and her lips parted to let him into the warm moistness.

His arms were suddenly no longer gentle. She was crushed to him as his mouth demanded her response; his hands explored downward over her straight back, and her curved hips were lifted into the hardness of his body. A deep growl in his throat turned to a moan as her arms went around him, her fingers digging into the hard muscle across his back.

Her hands dropped to his hips, pulling him closer. Her lips were free, and she was staring into light blue eyes half hidden by the thickness of dark lashes. Both of them had trouble with their breathing.

He shook his head. "It's been a long time, honey." A teasing light came into his eyes. "Hungry?"

"I don't think so. All I feel is giddy and uncoordinated." What she really wanted was to be held tightly to him just as he had been doing.

"You'll be suffering from jet lag several days. Besides, you've been traveling enough hours to need a good night's sleep without jet lag. Let's get these things off."

Once more, he pulled her close to him, slipping the jacket from her shoulders, unbuttoning the pearl buttons on her blouse. Docilely, she allowed him to undress her, leaning on him when he pulled her around, straightening when he pushed her one way or the other.

When she stood before in nothing but a skimpy bra and panty hose that enticed exploring fingers rather than hid her slimness, he looked only a moment before he swung her up into his arms. He strode down the hall, entering an open door to his right.

Her eyes flew open as he placed her on the big bed, and she felt it move to fit her body. He smiled and said softly, "Yes, it's a water bed. I ordered it especially for you."

She was thinking of the first bed they owned—a king-sized water bed they enjoyed in the first exploration of married sex, way back when they were young. He lay beside her, fully dressed, but he pulled the quilted coverlet over her as he held her. She moved as close to him as his clothing allowed.

"Russ?" Her question was muted against his throat.

"Yes?" The softness of his answer belied the tightness of his body as he responded to the smell and feel of the woman in his arms.

"Do you—do you want to—?" Her voice quit.

"Yes, I want to." Deep in his chest, she felt rather than heard his chuckle as his big hands fit over her hips.

"Let me—"

He interrupted. "Later, April. You're so tired you'd be asleep before I was through with you. When you give yourself to me, I want you to know you're getting me in return."

Her breathing was beginning to slow down. "But Russ, I want to—"

"I know. Go to sleep for now." He urged her close to him, and even in her half sleep, she felt through his clothing his body respond to his controlled desire for her. Smiling, she let the drifting sleep overtake her and gave herself up to the exhaustion of the trip.

THE STRANGENESS of her surroundings came through to her even though the room was dark. The smell was different. She could hear breathing, and her eyes searched the dimness for Brush. And then she remembered.

She was lying on her left side, her right hand along the edge of the bed. Pushing herself over, she turned on her back, easing her head over on the pillow. As her eyes grew accustomed to the darkness, the outline of another body was plainly visible, far away on the other side of the big bed. Russ lay an arm's length away from her.

Her breath caught audibly. She was in Sydney, with Russ, in a strange land, a strange house. With Russ. Her body still felt useless to her, and she stirred, sliding her legs across the space that separated them.

Rolling slightly, she fitted her body into the angles of Russ's hard muscular frame. Her fingers slid lightly across his bare hip, rubbing into the light layer of wiry hair.

"Are you asleep?" she whispered, making tiny kisses up his back to his shoulder.

For a moment he didn't answer; then a big hand closed over hers to pull it around him, placing it across his belly.

"Oh," she said.

"I'm awake," he said, and turned to pull her into his arms.

His hands went over her body, touching the curves and the crevices individually. She couldn't see his expression in the darkness, but she knew exactly when his breathing changed, and her fingers, spread across his chest, felt the heavy thud of his heartbeat.

Exploring hands returned to cup her breasts, and he moved his head downward, kissing from the fluttering pulse at the base of her throat to the shallow crevice between the two firm mounds. The tip of his tongue flicked gently at the brown tip, finally drawing it into his mouth.

She gasped. Liquid fire flowed, following the path he made to the other side with identical strokes of the plundering tongue, rousing the sleeping excitement within her. They were no longer sleepy or tired. Her body jerked with each caress.

Moaning, she tried to pull away from him, relenting to move closer and closer until there was nowhere for him to go except inside her.

Gently rolling her body, he followed, raising himself up on his knees. "Darling?" His hands were on each side of her now, and he lowered his mouth to touch hers. "Is it all right? Are you awake enough to know this is for real, that I love you and I want to take you for my own. Completely, April. Give me all of you."

As his whispered words asked the questions, her body reacted to the passion in his every move and word. Lifting her hips to meet him, she breathed her answer as he penetrated the soft moistness of her body. His hands cupped her buttocks, forcing her upward to meet his rapidly increasing strokes.

"I—honey?" His mouth came hard on hers, smothering her outcry, his tongue thrusting and retreating in perfect unison with their plunging, twisting bodies. The bursting explosion of white hot passion, denied for too long, rocked them with the floating sensation created by the water bed.

Wrapped in his arms, she lay contented for the moment. She smiled, rubbing her cheek across his hairy chest. "You're so sexy," she murmured.

If possible, his arms tightened. They didn't talk; there was no need just yet, no need for words to heal past hurts, no need for words to plan for the future. It was there for them when they needed it.

"Are we going to get married?" she asked, rousing herself from almost falling asleep again.

"Do you want to?" he asked. His voice was teasing. "Or would you like to just live like this?"

"Like what?"

"Spending a lot of time in this bed without benefit of being married. What if you *did* get pregnant? What then?"

"I don't know. Is there a possibility?"

"Only when you're ready, darling. Not until then." He pushed her head back on the pillow, still unable to see her face clearly. "Yes, we're getting married. As soon as it's possible. That means next week. Here a blood test is required, but the company doctor can take care of that for us."

He kissed her cheek, touching her ear as he went to her throat to lick gently along the long line of pale flesh. She quivered and felt his laugh against her body.

"Can we use the marriage license you bought in the States?" she asked. "I brought it with me."

He pulled away to look at her. "I wondered what happened to it. I never could find it after—" He stopped. "I'm sorry, honey. I'm so sorry." He eased her back into his arms, cuddling her, caressing the smoothness of her skin.

She knew what he was saying, and she nodded without speaking. She, too, was sorry. They had wasted a lot of time. Maybe not, she corrected her thoughts. Maybe we grew up and found out what real love is. We found each other again, and that's what counts above all.

With a long sigh of contentment, she relaxed and went to sleep, leaving Russ awake to hold her, thinking almost the same thoughts, wishing he could tell her how much he really loved her.

He smiled to himself just as sleep took over. Someday. Someday she'll know.

Epilogue

She finished her letters and started to the closet for the all-weather coat that had proved to be a much-needed item this time of year in Sydney. The general consensus of the local populace was that it was never *that* cold, but to April, a product of the California mildness, it was damp and cold. It went through her slender body as though she weren't even there.

The sound of a key turning in the lock stopped her in mid-stride, and she drew in her breath in surprise, glancing at her watch. It wasn't time for Russ to be coming in today. He had been out to the plant, and she didn't expect him back until quite a bit later.

"April?"

The surprise in her face was replaced by a smile as she started across the room. The door opened before she reached it, and Russ stood there. In his arms was Brush. Seeing her, he wriggled so hard Russ almost lost his hold on him.

"Oh! Oh, Brush, you're home!" She held out her hands, grasping the excited dog, receiving kisses punctuated with soft yips as she squeezed him.

Russ reached and pulled her into his arms, having to accept the dog with her. "I brought him home. Don't I get a welcome, too?"

She laughed, stooping to let Brush down, turning back to lean against him. "I wasn't expecting you so early. I haven't even started dinner."

"We can go out and eat."

"Brush won't allow us out of his sight so soon," she told him, her lips moving lightly over his chin, rough with the day's growth of beard.

"We can go to a drive-in," he teased her. "And have a hotdog."

She put her finger on his mouth. "Shh. Brush might hear you."

Hearing his name, Brush returned from his exploring, sitting near them in hopes of gaining some attention after being away so long. She complied, pulling away from Russ to kneel in front of the little dog to murmur pet talk to him.

As he calmed down and went to hop on the couch, Russ reached for her again. "Do you know what today is?"

"What?" She frowned. "It's Thursday. I have no idea what date it is."

"You've been here a month today," he said, punctuating the words with a kiss to each eye, down her nose, hovering just over her lips, his breath filling her with warmth.

"Hmm-mmm," she murmured, remembering. She moved closer.

They had married three weeks ago, with Webb Lewis and his wife going with them to the civil court as witnesses. His boss gave him two weeks off for a honeymoon, and Russ had spent that time convincing her she had made the right choice.

They didn't go anywhere but for the most part stayed in the warm friendliness of the terrace house, getting reacquainted. She tilted her head back to look into his face, seeing the desire flare in his eyes at the touch of her body, undulating slowly against him.

During the short periods she was out of his arms, he taught her the rules of the road for driving in Australia. The company furnished him with a car, so they didn't have to buy one. It was small and easy for her to handle after driving a rig for so many years.

Russ mentioned her job one evening as he lay on the couch, his head in her lap. "Will you be bored not working, April?" he asked. His eyes were closed, and she couldn't tell if he were serious.

Her fingers laced into his hair, pulling sharply, and she was rewarded with his grimace as his eyes flew open. "What's that for?"

She bent to press her lips into the thick gray-streaked hair she had yanked to get his attention. "It's my understanding they'd rather American citizens not take jobs the natives need," she told him.

He nodded, watching her. "I know, but you've always been so busy, I wasn't sure how you'd feel staying home waiting for me all the time."

"I don't intend to stay home and wait for you all the time," she replied, letting her finger slide into his ear, lightly going in and out of the opening.

He squeezed his eyes shut tightly, showing the edge of dark lashes, and his lips parted. Russ was affected by deep emotion when he did that, and she watched him, smiling. His ears, she had found, were love points to him, and he could be aroused easily by her touch there.

"Then what do you plan to do?" His voice was barely audible as she continued to play around his ear.

"Mrs. Lewis does volunteer work at the orphanage on the outskirts of the city, and she says they need a lot of people. I think I'd like that."

She looked down into his now wide-open eyes, seeing exactly what she wanted to see. They were filled with love, with wanting her, with desire fanned by her touch and the love reflected in the darkness of her eyes, in her soft mouth, shaped to fit his as she bent closer.

Suddenly, he sat up, turning to slide off the couch, pulling her with him. Without a break in his hold around her, he kissed her hard, lifting her body to fit over his. They had showered earlier and wore only robes, easy to be pushed aside, to gain access to each other.

"Honey," he murmured, "you're so sweet. You set me on fire." He broke off as her mouth settled over his, and she bit his lower lip, sucking it into her mouth, letting it go to catch the upper one, running her tongue underneath it until he moaned helplessly.

As he took her slowly, pushing her hips downward into his thighs, she opened her eyes to gaze into his face. Where fires once burned, a new flame had started. A flame destined to burn forever.

HARLEQUIN

FIRST·CLASS
Sweepstakes

OFFICIAL RULES

1. NO PURCHASE NECESSARY. To enter, complete the official entry/order form. Be sure to indicate whether or not you wish to take advantage of our subscription offer.

2. Entry blanks have been preselected for the prizes offered. Your response will be checked to see if you are a winner. In the event that these preselected responses are not claimed, a random drawing will be held from all entries received to award not less than $150,000 in prizes. This is in addition to any free, surprise or mystery gifts which might be offered. Versions of this sweepstakes with different prizes will appear in Preview Service Mailings by Harlequin Books and their affiliates. Winners selected will receive the prize offered in their sweepstakes brochure.

3. This promotion is being conducted under the supervision of Marden-Kane, an independent judging organization. By entering the sweepstakes, each entrant accepts and agrees to be bound by these rules and the decisions of the judges, which shall be final and binding. Odds of winning in the random drawing are dependent upon the total number of entries received. Taxes, if any, are the sole responsibility of the prize winners. Prizes are nontransferable. All entries must be received by August 31, 1986.

4. The following prizes will be awarded:

   (1) Grand Prize: Rolls-Royce™ *or* $100,000 Cash!
   (Rolls-Royce being offered by permission of Rolls-Royce Motors Inc.)

   (1) Second Prize: A trip for two to Paris for 7 days/6 nights. Trip includes air transportation on the Concorde, hotel accommodations...PLUS...$5,000 spending money!

   (1) Third Prize: A luxurious Mink Coat!

5. This offer is open to residents of the U.S. and Canada, 18 years or older, except employees of Harlequin Books, its affiliates, subsidiaries, Marden-Kane and all other agencies and persons connected with conducting this sweepstakes. All Federal, State and local laws apply. Void in the province of Quebec and wherever prohibited or restricted by law. Winners will be notified by mail and may be required to execute an affidavit of eligibility and release, which must be returned within 14 days after notification. Canadian winners will be required to answer a skill-testing question. Winners consent to the use of their name, photograph and/or likeness for advertising and publicity purposes in conjunction with this and similar promotions without additional compensation. One prize per family or household.

6. For a list of our most current prize winners, send a stamped, self-addressed envelope to: WINNERS LIST, c/o Marden-Kane, P.O. Box 10404, Long Island City, New York 11101

She fought for a bold future until she could no longer ignore the...

ECHO OF THUNDER

MAURA SEGER

Author of **Eye of the Storm**

ECHO OF THUNDER is the love story of James Callahan and Alexis Brockton, who forge a union that must withstand the pressures of their own desires and the challenge of building a new television empire.

Author Maura Seger's writing has been described by *Romantic Times* as having a "superb blend of historical perspective, exciting romance and a deep and abiding passion for the human soul."

The final book in the trilogy by

MAURA SEGER

EDGE OF DAWN

The story of the Callahans and Garganos concludes as Matthew and Tessa must stand together against the forces that threaten to destroy everything their families have built.

From the unrest and upheaval of the sixties and seventies to the present, *Edge of Dawn* explores a generation's coming of age through the eyes of a man and a woman determined to love no matter what the cost.

COMING IN FEBRUARY 1986

EDG-H-1

You're invited to accept 4 books and a surprise gift Free!

Acceptance Card

Mail to: Harlequin Reader Service®

In the U.S.	In Canada
2504 West Southern Ave.	P.O. Box 2800, Postal Station A
Tempe, AZ 85282	5170 Yonge Street
	Willowdale, Ontario M2N 6J3

YES! Please send me 4 free Harlequin American Romance® novels and my free surprise gift. Then send me 4 brand new novels as they come off the presses. Bill me at the low price of $2.25 each —an 11% saving off the retail price. There are no shipping, handling or other hidden costs. There is no minimum number of books I must purchase. I can always return a shipment and cancel at any time. Even if I never buy another book from Harlequin, the 4 free novels and the surprise gift are mine to keep forever.

154 BPA-BPGE

Name   (PLEASE PRINT)

Address   Apt. No.

City   State/Prov.   Zip/Postal Code

This offer is limited to one order per household and not valid to present subscribers. Price is subject to change.   ACAR-SUB-1

Readers rave about
Harlequin American Romance!

"...the best series of modern romances
I have read...great, exciting, stupendous,
wonderful."
> —S.E.* Coweta, Oklahoma

"...they are absolutely fantastic...going to be
a smash hit and hard to keep on the
bookshelves."
> —P.D., Easton, Pennsylvania

"The American line is great. I've enjoyed
every one I've read so far."
> —W.M.K., Lansing, Illinois

"...the best stories I have read in a long
time."
> —R.H., Northport, New York

*Names available on request.